BLOOD LOTTO

BLOOD LOTTO

Greg Caldwell

BLOOD LOTTO

ACKNOWLEDGMENT

This book is dedicated to the memory of my parents, Captain Merle F. 'Bud' Caldwell and Winnie Caldwell for their love and inspiration. They will always be with me.

I want to thank my wife, Tracy, my children, Ashley, Eric, and my friends for their support and contributions in creating this book. I also wish to thank Tammy Barnett for her awesome editing skills of this book.

C H A P T E R 1

2073

I watch in horror as the U.N. military police fire their weapons into a crowd of starving poorly armed citizens. The tension has been building all day, as has the demand for food distribution from this government repository. People begin to scream as several Columbian citizens, too close to escape, fall backwards from the bullets' impact. Panic engulfs the large crowd as everyone pushes backwards to escape the sudden barrage. Blood sprays from deep wounds as the bullets hit their marks. The explosions of gunfire and the screams from the crowd ring in my ears with a deafening tone. The once angry mob dissolves quickly into a terror-stricken stampede.

I yell at the top of my lungs, "Stop firing! These people only need their food!" My shrieks are drowned out by the screaming. A feeling of panic pulses over me as the scene only continues to worsen.

I look quickly to my left, noticing a woman clutching an infant. She's doing her best to run for cover as the crowd begins to shove her backwards. I push through the crowd in order to reach her before she falls. The terror on people's faces as they scramble and shove around me is unforgettable. My progress is frustrating as I keep losing sight of her. If she falls, the crowd will trample both of them to death.

Suddenly, I see her tumble, clutching the infant to her chest. She hunches down to protect the baby from harm as she collapses to her knees. The crowd continues to trample around her.

I again scream, louder, "Someone help that lady!" It is hopeless. Everyone is too terror stricken to notice.

I continue to shove my way towards her, aggressively maneuvering through the crowd. My heart pounds as I make my way to the area where she has fallen. I hear the zing of a bullet pass over my head, intensifying the danger. A feeling of total helplessness begins to engulf me as I silently pray for an end to this madness. Lunging forward, I catch a glimpse of the mother lying in a heap. She is huddling over the child to protect the baby from being killed. Pushing people aside, I kneel down to her. Both of them are alive but shaken badly. I get her to her feet in the midst of the chaos. People continue to scramble around us as the weapons discharge. It takes all her effort, but we finally make it to a place of safety behind a building. She's badly banged up, but alive. The baby remains unhurt. As traumatized as she is, she still manages to smile as she holds onto my hand.

I can hear her mutter, "Dios Le Bendice (God bless you)," as a tear rolls down her face.

Smoke from the gunpowder begins to appear in the air. I look around the corner from the building to witness dozens of bodies lying in front of the repository. The road begins to show small canals of blood.

I hear a lieutenant yell to his troops, "Cease fire! Cease fire!"

As quickly as the gunfire began, the shooting stops. The sudden silence is only temporary as moans and cries from survivors begin to fill the air. I step from behind the building noticing at least forty people shot or trampled. Most of them lie motionless as the life force drains from their bodies.

The same lieutenant raises a megaphone to his mouth, "You people were told to disburse until the orders came to release this food. You bring this conflict upon yourselves. Take care of your dead and wounded. An announcement will be made when these supplies will be released."

I watch these poor people return to the aid of their loved ones. A few of the victims still cling to life as they moan from the pain. The guards remain in formation. None lend a hand to the people they have just targeted. If I had a weapon in my hands, I would open up on all of them. This massacre is catastrophic. I have to fight the rage that rumbles within me.

The temperature and humidity of the day is getting to intolerable levels. Everyone is moving slowly as the trauma of this tragedy sinks in. Sweat begins to run down my face as I assist with the casualties. We move the dead to a temporary morgue. A few of the survivors are taken away to a nearby clinic. Their hopes of survival are slim here in this forgotten part of the world. Proper medicines and medical care are nearly nonexistent.

A Columbian national stands up from the body of a dead loved one and begins to shout in his native tongue, "I will see to it that all you pay for my brother's murder! This I promise to you!"

The guards hold their positions without flinching. I pray this man doesn't provoke them again. Enough blood has been shed on this land. A woman, probably his wife, pleads with him to quiet down and leave with her. He hesitates but walks with her in a state of rage.

This whole incident exploded when someone from the crowd threw a bottle at the guards. Most of these people had not eaten a decent meal in weeks. The provisions were supposed to be distributed at nine a.m., but because of bureaucratic bullshit the distribution became delayed. My job is to help distribute this food properly and keep records for the supplier. The guards should have let us hand the supplies out on time. The military will have to suffer the consequences of this catastrophe.

The food here in Columbia, South America has been dwindling steadily over the past several years. My heart really goes out to these people who just gathered here today to get their fair share of rations. Third world countries like South America have been affected drastically from the population overload. This food shortage is not impacting the more domesticated countries quite as intensely.

It's hours before I make it back to my bungalow. The food finally got disbursed when the guards released the supplies. I don't remember feeling as fatigued as I do now. Walking over to a partially cracked mirror, I gaze at my reflection. I don't like what I see. The face that reflects back is almost unrecognizable. The partial grey showing in my moustache and sideburns, along with a few new lines in my face demonstrate how much torment these last few years have been. I was considered a ladies' man. My light brown hair is tragically in need of a haircut. The old scar on my forehead is the only facial feature that's fading. I'm really getting worn out with all this shit. Trying to do some good in the world may just get me killed one day. Here I sit in this hell hole of a third world country while even the politicians don't give a damn about these people.

I have to hear what the media is broadcasting. The television snaps on as I click the remote control. A reporter is describing the events that just occurred.

"The death toll from this horrendous onslaught has reached forty-three. The United Nations Government has made no comment as to the actions of its military unit here in Columbia. This savage attack on ordinary unarmed citizens is inexcusable. With the growing necessity for food distribution in areas such as this, the government continues to fail in its efforts to feed the ever growing population. The food necessary to feed all of the citizens worldwide becomes more scarce every day. Until a solution manifests itself, more situations such as this will continue to occur."

I can't listen to anymore. I already know the outcome. This reporter's right, the military had no business firing into a crowd of people. The U.N. would brush this under the rug just the way they cover up everything else.

Since the year 2060, the world has really fallen apart. The population just keeps increasing without the proper amount of food to feed everyone. This shortage isn't affecting the more civilized countries as intensely. Many restaurants and food centers within North America and Europe still remain open. Food and supplies just can't reach the outer regions.

A knock at the door rattles me to my senses. It must be my partner, Mike Coats, who accompanied me on this trip.

"Let me inside, before I get ambushed waiting out here in the street," Mike grumbles as he clears his throat from behind the door.

Fumbling with the lock I manage to unlatch the door. "I'm glad you made it out of there alive. What's going on out there?"

"I got held up while trying to get this damn government employee to release more of the food. It's all politics and red damn tape! Food supplies are getting scarce down here and our supplier can't increase the shipments right now. We're in a cluster fuck."

Mike's complexion is beat red under his four-day beard growth. The humidity outside is taking its toll on him. His shirt is stained from the sweat of the day as he staggers, ready to collapse from the heat. The door slams shut behind him.

"This jobs becoming impossible!" I bark, remembering today's incident. "There just isn't enough food to go around anymore. I've been hearing rumors that the U.N. may have to cut off certain areas from receiving food all together."

Mike looks at me with a serious expression, "It's going to happen unless they come up with a better system. They just can't keep feeding this many people. It's only the year 2073 and we can't even produce enough food to go around." He finally plunks down on a rickety chair. "I've heard rumors lately that the U.N. has been discussing an alternative solution, and will announce it soon."

"Nothing is worse than watching helpless people get massacred for just demanding food handouts." I nod my head in disgust.

Mike looks the room over for a bite to eat as sweat trickles down his face. "I'm tired of being in some damn kill zone area of the world. This damn heat is going to kill me before anything else."

"Don't count on this government having a quick fix. They can't even disperse the food properly."

"Tony, I'm serious. I've heard rumors that a committee has been formed by the United Nations to make drastic changes in the population. I don't know what they have up their sleeves, but it can't be good."

Attempting to keep the weariness out of my voice, "Tomorrow will be another day, and the both of us will be out of here on a plane back to the States."

The musty moldy smell of the room emphasizes my anxiousness to leave this rotten place. A worn out, stained mattress to rest my head on doesn't help matters. The floor boards creak and rattle with every step from years of use. I do feel lucky as most people in this part of the world have to sleep in grass huts. Some of them don't even have this luxury available to them.

The world has really changed these last forty years, especially since the United Nations took over as a global government. It is now the year 2073, and problems worldwide have really compounded themselves. Since the year 2065, the over-population problem has been a key issue for the government to resolve. Dramatic laws have been passed such as preselected infant castration, and voluntary surgical castration of young adults for a monetary payment. A zero population growth could not be obtained no matter what the government did. The population has increased at an alarming rate, reaching 10.5 billion people and unfortunately without a comparable increase in the food production worldwide. If you are lucky enough to live in a country with plenty of resources, life is tolerable.

The General Assembly of the United Nations in its original innovation had proclaimed a Universal Declaration of Human Rights that protected everyone. These rights were abandoned when the U.N. took over as the world government. The dignity and respect of the original preamble needs to be restored to its original protections.

Starvation has become misery for many people who live on a diet of insects, rats, and any animal or plant that can be consumed. The government has been taking over most of the distribution of the main food supply globally in an attempt to even out this apportionment. As the company I am working for is discovering, food distribution is in complete chaos. We monitor issuance in an attempt to ensure that the food ends up in the hands and stomachs of the most deserving. Today's bloody massacre is the last straw for me, and proof that this system does not work. It's becoming obvious that soon my own death will be inevitable if I keep working as a distribution contractor. My grave stone will read, 'Tony Fisher, killed while feeding the needy'.

Mike wearily spoke as he moves to an old mattress in the corner, "Sleep is the only thing I really need. I haven't had a good night's sleep since I got here. This damn humidity will kill a person before starvation takes them."

I inquire to hear how Mike feels about today's military action, "You should have seen the terror in the faces of these people today. The military just opened up on them like they were shooting at paper targets. None of them had a chance. If a lieutenant hadn't stopped them, a hundred or more of them would have been put in the grave."

"They'll have to pay the price for that screw up. I'll just be damn glad to get the hell out of here tomorrow. I believe this government is sending out the wrong message to everyone," Mike stops for a second to yawn. "They want to make sure everyone knows they have the upper hand," He continues to mutter as he rolls over to get more comfortable.

I opt to inform Mike, "I'm going to stay in California a few days when our flight lands tomorrow. I'll catch up with you later in the week in D.C. I've got some personal matters to attend to."

He clears his throat with a yawn and replies, "If anyone deserves some time off, you do. Take as much time as you need. I'll cover for you. Just remember, there's going to be a lot of damn paper work to complete on this one."

"Ah, people dying in the trenches always creates more paperwork," I sarcastically reply. "The lives of these people mean a lot more to me than a batch of paper work. Get some sleep. I'll talk to you about it in the morning." I had to close my mouth before my anger got the best of me.

"Ten four, good buddy," Mike babbles in a semi-conscious state of sleep.

I begin to wrestle with a lot of thoughts, as I lay awake in the steamy humid room. This job is really getting to me, and my partner doesn't seem to give a damn whether people died today or not. I really can't go back to work for this company. What was I accomplishing anyways? Maybe things will be clearer in the morning. This government is about to make an announcement regarding a new policy they had been secretly discussing. Maybe it will help things out, and bring about a better system for us.

I suddenly feel something crawling up my leg. Springing to my feet, I witness the largest roach I have ever laid my eyes on. With a quick snap of my wrist, I send the slimy creature sailing to the other side of the room, about where Mike is sleeping. I hope the two of them will have a great night together. I'm done trying to get any sleep in this bug-infested, humid, slimy excuse for a bungalow. The sun is beginning to break through the window, and today I will finally get out of this jungle.

Mike begins to squirm a bit as he throws back a partially stained sheet, "Something's crawling around over here by my feet!"

"It could be that ugly senorita you were trying to pick up yesterday. Seems like she wanted you." I laugh knowing the roach has found a new snack to munch on. "Better get up. The jeeps going to be here to pick us up in less than an hour. We need to get to the airstrip on time."

Every time I have an assignment with Mike, he always makes a fool of himself trying to pick up younger girls. His poor choice in women always lands him in more trouble than he can handle. The roach may be the best date he will find on this trip.

His voice increases an octave, "I would have been sleeping with her last night if all that trouble hadn't started."

"Yeah Mike…and my grandmothers going to be our next U.N. president," I jest with an air of indifference.

"Laugh all you want. She was really digging on me."

"Look the jeep's pulling up right now. Get your ass up or stay in this Columbian jungle."

It is the fastest I've ever seen Mike move. Like a Thorough bred horse on a track, he's out the door. His sightly chubby torso never misses a beat, as he grabs up his belongings and gets them into the jeep.

Looking around the room, I yell out to him, "Are you sure you got everything?"

"As much as I need. Let's get to that airstrip."

I climb into the jeep, pulling my bags in with me. The driver is in desperate need of a shower and a change of clothes, judging by the odor my olfactory senses pick up. His unkept beard and dirt-stained hands tells me we are in for a wild ride to the plane. His nervous behavior gives me an uneasy feeling. It's the only way to the airstrip, so I'm not about to stir up trouble. From the moment we drive off, his speed is off the charts especially for this kind of rocky road. His first corner almost tips the jeep over. The tires skip and slide sideways as he accelerates into the corner.

"What's the hurry? I want to arrive at the plane in one piece!" I nervously ask.

He gives me a serious side glance, "People here won't hesitate to jump a jeep like this one. Just to get anything we may be carrying. If they need it…they'll take it."

"Desperate times, desperate actions. It's like that?" Mike mutters as he glances into the jungle terrain we pass.

"It's just like that! Two or three got hit just last week. Killed three people just to get the food they had," the driver blasts back to Mike as we skid around another curve.

"Maybe we should have gotten a military escort to get us to the airstrip," Mike states in a jittery voice.

The driver slaps his leg and snorts with a strange kind of laugh, "You won't get any escorts from this military. They won't do shit for anybody. Look how many they put in the grave yesterday." Having only one hand on the steering wheel, he almost runs us off the road. He fights to keep the jeep on the rough roadway.

I remain silent at his remark. Yesterday is a day I wish to forget. It won't be in my memoirs as one of my most favorite days. I have to confess, this rough poorly educated man rationalizes a good point. The military does nothing for these people.

As we make another corner, I catch a glimpse of the airstrip to my right. It's a grand sight to behold, as the jungle seems to be closing in on us. I notice a few military guards at the gate guarding the airstrip. I'm glad to see them, even though the driver has doubts about their usefulness.

"Well, looks like you fellas got lucky today. The food handouts they got yesterday must have fed the locals last night. Things might just be good for a few days," the driver informs us with his seasoned intelligence as we pull through the gate.

"I can't say I blame them, especially when they're starving to death. Ask yourself, how you would react in their situation?" I inquire to the driver.

He gives a shrug of his shoulders, implying with an indifference on the question. We wind through the gate as a guard motions us on through. Noticing the plane on the runway, my apprehension lifts a bit. Activity is developing around the plane as we pull up. The guards have an individual, probably a Columbian national, pinned down in a spread-eagle position near the plane. Three of the guards are standing with rifles locked on him, ready to fire if given the order. I jump out of the vehicle after it stops. The individual on the ground is begging in his Columbian dialect, with beads of sweat rolling off his forehead, in an attempt to persuade the guards to release him. His hands are tied behind his back with a rope that is stretched down also lashing his feet. The plane is running with the pilot and co-pilot at the controls. A few people are on board waiting for our arrival.

I inquire of one of the guards, "What did this man do?"

A guard holding some papers and a satchel answers, "This is a military matter. He was caught trying to sneak on the plane as a stowaway. Don't get involved, just get on the plane."

Mike walks up with his baggage in hand, "Don't shoot him until we get off the ground. I don't like the sight of blood."

"I hope you don't shoot him at all. If I were him, I'd try to leave this place any way I could," I comment quickly, giving Mike a dirty look.

"I told you, it's a military matter and don't involve yourself," The guard sternly remarks.

I glance over to the driver of the jeep. As he pulls away, I see him give me a half wave as if to signal me; I told you so.

"I hope you give the man a break." I add as a last plea.

The guards ignore my comment and continue to talk among themselves. Mike and I climb up the few steps to the open door of the plane. I look back at the Columbian national whose fate is up for grabs. I can only partially imagine how they will punish him for such a simple crime. How many years will they lock him up for? I continue into the plane locating a baggage compartment to store my belongings. I locate a seat to sit down in as the plane begins to taxi toward the runway. The engines increase in rpm's as the pilot throttles the controls.

I give Mike a pitiful stare, "Why would you suggest to those guards to shoot that poor Columbian?"

Mike shrugs his shoulders in a stupid sort of way, "I just didn't feel like seeing any blood before the flight. Anyways they aren't going to shoot that man. They already have him tied up like a Christmas gift."

Suddenly, two shots ring out from behind the plane as we taxi away from the guards. I look quickly out the side window towards the area. Blood is trickling out the head of the man we just saw strapped on the ground. A slight haze of smoke is hovering around the weapons the guards hold. I don't believe what I am seeing!

"Take a good look Mike! Maybe your conscience doesn't bother you, but mine bothers the hell out of me!" Mike's indifference is the final blow.

Mike stares back at the scene with a look of total shock on his face, "I didn't think they would really do it!"

Sitting back in my chair with my eyes closed is the only solitude I can achieve. I can feel that sudden sensation of weightlessness as the plane leaves the runway. The sound of the engines humming is therapeutic, as I slip into a state of needed sleep.

I suddenly awaken by the jolt of the plane striking the ground. Opening my eyes, I look at my watch and find that five hours have passed. The flight must be landing in California, as the scenery out the window looks familiar. I gaze over at Mike with his mouth half open sleeping in the chair next to me.

"Get up Mike. You need to catch a connecting flight to D.C. in forty minutes."

He jerks awake as the plane engines wind down to a taxiing speed. He looks out the window as if the scenery is a dream he has concocted, "Man, civilization at last. I hope I never have to go back to Columbia again. For any reason."

I yell to Mike as I grab my bag and quickly walk toward the exit, "Keep your butt out of trouble." I flash him a half wave as I make it through the door of the plane. I'm positive I will not see him again. I've made a decision to quit this job as quickly as I can get to a phone. I'm tired of finding myself in these rotten situations without a decent partner to count on.

The Los Angeles airport is just as congested and crowded as ever. However, it's great to be back in the States again given the past week I've endured. I look up to a monitor in the baggage area as a U.N. presidential news broadcast is being announced, interrupting the local station. It's the announcement the government has been planning to make regarding the population control regulations. I step closer to the monitor to listen to the broadcast.

"From the Presidential Office in Iceland, I give you the president of the United Nations, Jarmine Meranse." The president steps up to the microphone, "I am honored to speak to you today on a matter of such great importance. We have spent years passing regulations and laws pertaining to our most intense problem facing the world today. Overpopulation. The world's population continues to grow in spite of regulations that have been administered to retard this growth. A United Nations Regulation Committee formed three years ago to discuss with government leaders around the world and myself a way to end this population growth that is causing so much starvation and torment. Increased food supplies and distribution is not sufficient to feed everyone, as the population continues to surpass these supplies. The situation yesterday, in Columbia, South America is a testament to the crisis we have reached. My sympathy and blessings are extended to those families and individuals that suffered through that situation. A delegate of this committee, Jordan Stanovich, has developed a solution for this population crisis. Today, with a saddened heart, I have passed this plan into law as a last resort to save our great planet from the perils of starvation.

A worldwide lottery will be held every three months on a global basis. Every country, island, and continent has been topographically sectioned off into grid areas containing approximately an even distribution of people. Ten-thousand grids across this globe have been carefully mapped out. This lottery will randomly select one grid every three months by computer. When an area has been chosen, prior to its announcement to the world, the United Nations Military Force will seal the borders and confine this population. No one will be allowed to leave it's borders. A gas has been developed to painlessly put these individuals to a permanent sleep at the end of one week.

Today is March 16th, 2073. The first lottery will be held approximately six months from today and continue every three months for three years. At that time, we will reevaluate the conditions in the world to justify the necessity to continue this lottery. I am saddened to make such an announcement to the world this day. It is with tremendous grief that I condemn individuals to save a greater populace. May God bless all of you, and save us from this catastrophe that faces the world today."

I can't believe what I have just heard. My mind is whirling, as I can't fully grasp the magnitude of the president's speech. The normal loud commotion of the airport becomes unusually silent. Looking into people's faces, I see the same shock that I feel. The unusual silence around me quickly changes instantly to a loud chatter. This must be some kind of hoax. This can't be the governments answer.

THE ANNOUNCEMENT

With the government's announcement, many people begin to panic. My own convictions could not condone the world's military ending the lives of innocent people. This government really crossed the line announcing such a grotesque solution. It almost seems surreal, as if the president's speech was imagined.

I've been on my own for fifteen years, spending a few of them in our New World Naval Services. I joined because of my love of the sea. It was an alright life, at least you got two square meals a day. When my term ended, I was ready to get out. Navy life is alright for some of the guys, but I'm always looking for that proverbial 'pot of gold at the end of the rainbow'. I made a lot of friends in the navy from all parts of the world. It didn't matter where you originated because your birthplace country only showed up as a patch on your jacket. A language barrier exists, but English is still the main language spoken. You either learn to speak English or you fall behind.

Joining the Navy had a few special perks. Our unit traveled a lot, so we got to visit areas of the world that only a few people can imagine. A location I will never forget is an island in the Caribbean. It has a very interesting layout and unique geological formations. Only a few of us know about this cavern. We discovered it totally by accident on maneuvers one day. Our unit was dispatched to the island to set it up as a recognizance area. We had time on our hands, so a few days of scuba diving around the island was a necessity. On the second day, three of us took a skip boat around to the far end of the island. These skip boats are fast and very well camouflaged. We found an area containing an array of strange cave formations about 85 to 95 feet down. Upon entering one of these caves, we discovered a large underwater cavern that left me speechless. The cavern bottoms out at a depth of approximately 200 feet, while the sides are easily 300 to 400 feet apart. As we surfaced within the cavern, a room opened up above the water line that was incredible!

The island was formed by volcanic lava. As the lava cooled, ocean water surged in to form large underwater caverns. As time passed, coral reefs grew, surrounding the cave with natural camouflage. A few strategically placed charges of dynamite at the opening could produce an underwater fortress of amazing capabilities. The sides of the cavern, above the water line, could accommodate housing for many, making it the perfect hideaway. All it would take is the manpower necessary to complete the job. Easily, it could be the hideaway of all hideaways. This huge room contained its own network of caves and passageways. Marine life is abundant, creating a great source of food. Many schools of Yellow Snapper, Tangs, Parrot fish, Sheepshead and others were plentiful. Occasional sharks moved in and around the cavern, waiting for a sporadic meal. The three of us, Kurt, Malik (a natural born Jamaican), and I made a pact not to disclose this location to anyone. I knew I could count on them. We nicknamed the island, 'Starpoint'.

My closest buddy from the Navy will be the first person I need to contact. He may be the craziest son of a bitch I ever met, but I know I can count on him for anything. His name is Kurt Lopez. He's part Navaho Indian and part Mexican-the other parts you can only guess. His physical build is quite extraordinary, and he usually maintains the strength of a bull elephant. I always tell him that his face is a dead ringer for 'Sitting Bull'. The lines in his face, and general bold Indian features make him a shoe-in for the part. His hair always remained black as charcoal and cut close in a military fashion.

On the last combat mission we fought together, Kurt demonstrated what a true lifesaver he really is. We were caught in a crossfire situation in South America and it seemed like the only way out would be our deaths. This son of a bitch pulls off one of the most miraculous stunts of the whole war. We remained pinned down by artillery fire from just about every direction. Most of our unit was either missing or dead. Seven of us fought our best just to see the next few minutes. The terrain was impossible containing mostly solid jungle and swamp fields. Kurt grabbed a grenade launcher and began to spray the surrounding area like a man possessed. He discovered the aim of a sharpshooter, landing those grenades right on the heads of sixteen Brazilian fighters to our south.

Three of our remaining seven men had been wounded from the last few hours of battle. One of them, Thomas Chess, had been hit in the right leg and right arm, severing vessels. The leg wound looked bad enough to keep him from walking for the rest of his life. We had a tourniquet tied, but the man was still losing a lot of blood. Kurt grabbed up Thomas and threw him over his shoulder like a sack of potatoes. He began to run into the jungle to our south while the rest of us followed.

Kurt kept up a barrage of grenades with his other free arm, yelling back at us, "This is the way out, boy's!" He managed to place the grenades strategically, taking out the enemy as we labored through the jungle. A normal man would have had trouble handling that gun with both hands, but Kurt managed to fire it with one arm while carrying a man across his shoulder with the other. I believe he made a pact with God because I never saw anything like it in my life! We all made it out that day thanks to some quick actions on Kurt's part. From that day forward, Kurt and I became the best of friends. If there is anyone, I know I can count on, it's Kurt.

Malik Isaacs, the Jamaican, is the second person I need to contact. He was the cut-up and jokester of our unit and made each day worth living. His strong Jamaican features and hair locks made his Jamaican heritage unmistakable. You never knew what to expect from this guy. One day he added some heavy laxative to a few pre-selected drinking containers used by the officers on board. The containers were delivered by a runner working for the commanding officer of our ship. Never has a ship stunk so bad! The commanding officer and fellow officers spent the night wishing they put ten times the number of toilets aboard. The whole affair got written off as bad food, but we all knew better. Together with his Jamaican tongue, you can't help but like the guy.

The time has come to locate a few friends and start making plans. Kurt Lopez will be my first contact. The last I heard, he is living in Cancun, Mexico. He likes the fact that the authorities do not bother him there. He says, "You have the freedom there you deserve!" I sent him an e-mail to see if he still resides there. I soon receive an answer. He writes, 'Come on down and join me in my bungalow! The water is fine, the women are spirted, and the party never stops!'

I need to go down there and really give him something to live for. What he really needs to wake up his spirit is a conflict. A buddy of mine in the navy gets me on a naval air-cargo escort flight to Cancun within a day.

In Cancun, I head down to the shipping docks where Kurt resides. The district is just about what I expect, with the normal hotels, and a few authentic Mexican buildings. Most people here seem to be struggling to make ends meet, similar to the United States. The bar he mentioned in his e-mail is just on the edge of the district, on a side street. It has a certain appeal, with an adobe color onto the front. In the window, I see a colorful neon parrot that flickers an exotic array of colors. The street is littered with trash, but I expect that in this district. I notice a few ladies of the evening walking further down the street. As I enter the doors of the bar, the first thing that catches my eye is Kurt. He is sitting at a table at the back edge of the bar having a drink. Two fairly sexy Mexican girls are sitting at the table with him. One of them is massaging Kurt's neck while the other one is talking to them.

He sees me come through the door and springs to his feet, yelling, "Here comes the pride of the Navy and the scum of the earth all rolled up in one!" Laughing, he runs across the bar, yanks me up on his shoulder, runs me back to his table, and plops me into a chair.

It's the same old Kurt, just as crazy as ever!

"You're looking good, partner!" I say.

"No! Not me. It's the ladies that are looking good!" Kurt boasts with a laugh. "You need a drink, amigo. Where's that bartender?"

Suddenly, a large Mexican gentlemen bursts through the door yelling, "I'll bust the heads of anyone I find with my daughter! Where is that little shit?" He stumbles around in a fury.

I look over, and the man is gazing right at us. This is great! I haven't been with Kurt for even five minutes and he already has me in trouble. I glance over at the girl sitting beside me at the table. She has a strange look of fear on her face. I know I'm in trouble now!

Kurt, in his lunatic wisdom, springs up quickly and yells, "Your daughter can't be in any trouble. She's been here with us all this time, protected by me and my buddy!"

Trouble is about to sting the two of us right in the ass. I stand up quickly, ready for the worst. The Mexican storms over to our table and squares himself off face to face with Kurt. Both of them stare at each other with looks that can kill! As I get up, ready to jump this big hombre, both of them begin to laugh like two hyenas. I've been had!

The Mexican gentlemen look over at me and begins to laugh even louder. It must be the stupid look on my face. The two of them almost collapse on the table laughing at my expense.

"Tony, Meet my friend. He owns this bar. This is Carlos Cortez," Kurt starts off with the introductions still laughing.

Carlos extends his massive hand out for me to shake, "Senor, It is good to meet you. Any friend of Kurts is a friend that needs help." His laugh explodes again as he continues to shake my hand. "Name your poison amigo. What can I pour you?"

Hoping he'll let go of my hand soon, I order, "Give me a scotch, straight up. You two sure know how to crunch a fellow!"

"Coming right up, and welcome to the Casa de' La Parrot bar." He stomps off still howling with laughter.

Kurt nudges me on the shoulder, "Tony, I want you to meet my wife, Adrian and my daughter, Liana."

"Partner, why haven't you told me you were married? You're one lucky hombre to have two beautiful girls to show off," I exclaim, as his introduction about knocks me off my chair. His wife stands about five-feet-four-inches tall with silky black hair that falls below her waist. Her complexion is dark tan with beautiful radiant eyes. The daughter is almost a dead ringer for her mom, in a youthful sort of way. The two of them together would stop any man in his tracks.

"Don't get any wild ideas, this one is taken, and my daughter is too young." Kurt snickers, still fueled from the caper.

"Well, you certainly have done well for yourself. I'm so glad to meet you lovely ladies."

The drinks flow for hours as we laugh, talk, and reminisce about old times. It is great to see him again. He has really made a great life for himself here. I'm almost hesitant to talk with him about the real reason I came to see him.

It takes me a few hours, but I finally get Kurt aside, "How do you feel about the world situation, in particular this lottery?"

"I never thought this government would come up with a crock of shit like this. This Stanovich needs a cattle prod shoved up his ass! What the hell are they thinking?"

"I'm glad you have a low opinion of the man who is about to commit mass murder of more innocent people. I was there when the military opened up on those people in Columbia. It was a pure massacre. None of them had a chance."

"What other opinion could someone have? You must have had a rough time down there."

"I need your help to stop this damn lottery! I'm not sure just yet how I plan to do it, but someone has to. A lot more innocent people will die, if we let them continue."

Kurt gives me a puzzled look, but he seems intrigued. I fill him in on a rough plan I have been thinking about. I remind him, "Remember that island in the Caribbean we found? It could be the perfect central pivot point for an operation. I know a lot of work needs to go into it, but its location and resources are perfect. I'll bet with the proper number of people to work on it, we can have it together in about two months." Kurt listens as if every word renews him within.

I outline my plan. "We have got to organize an underground rebellion. We need to form a network of carefully chosen people that can help us stop this madness. We will have to get organized quickly, so no possibility exists of information leaking out."

Kurt answers quickly, "You know I'm in, amigo. I just don't know how we start up an organization like this. Outside of my military training, I haven't organized a damn thing. You need to let me know how we are going to find the proper people."

I fill him in on a list of people I have in mind for strategic importance. "We need to get a hold of Jimmy Turner. You remember Jimmy: He was the demolition expert in our old naval unit. He'll be able to open up that cavern in a heartbeat. We also can't forget about Malik Isaacs, who could probably get us most of the odd things we will need. He can bullshit anybody out of anything, and he already knows about the cavern!"

I have to ask, "How are you going to break the news to your wife and daughter? I hope they go along with it."

"Adrian is rebellious in nature anyways. She will jump at the chance to shut down this bullshit lottery. I'll make some plans, so Liana won't be in danger. She is a tough little girl, but this type of thing is not what she needs."

"I won't have it any other way," I answer.

Kurt also adds, "Besides owning this bar, Carlos knows many people in this area having access to information and goods. What we could really use is a submarine to get us to that island. One that is large enough for equipment transfer. We can trust him. I know him like a brother. I'll talk to him in the morning."

"There's just one drawback." He leans close to me as he whispers, "We probably will have to steal one. Unless you have one in your back pocket?"

We stay up most of the night making plans and brainstorming details. I knew I could count on Kurt, I just hope it's not the booze in him talking.

CHAPTER 3

THE OPERATION

I wake up feeling very hung over but extremely excited about the conversations and enthusiasm we had last night. Adrian is the only one awake, and I hear her rattling around in the kitchen. It may be a good time to talk with her about the sudden changes in her life. She has a pot of coffee going, anticipating the hang overs we are waking up to. She pours me a cup.

I inquire, "I know all of this must be a shock to you. I hope you can understand how important it is we stop this lottery."

She looks at me for a second replying, "Let me tell you about my childhood. Then you will understand how I feel."

She explains, "When I was ten years old, Mexico was run by Santiago Tomez, a dictator that was corrupt in most of his affairs. My father was a landowner and rancher who had inherited this land from his father. Our ranch was over 300 acres of the most fertile land in the territory. Santiago decided that this land was too good for the present landowner, so he decided to take the land from my father. My dad was angery and wouldn't sign the property over to him. Santiago sent his henchmen out to my father's house one night, and they beat my father to death! The land was confiscated, and my mother and I were run off. I made a pact with God, never to allow someone to rob and destroy my family ever again."

"Since then, Santiago has died, but this man Jordan Stanovich is worse than Santiago could ever be. I will fight to the death to stop the madness of this lottery! I hope now you can see how grateful I am to have you here. Kurt is a good man, and has always been a great husband and father. I will go wherever Kurt wants me to go!"

I remain silent for a moment, unable to imagine the pain she must have gone through. I look into her sad eyes and with my next breath exclaim, "I promise we will do everything in our power to stop what is happening. I give you my word!" I suggest, "I want Liana and you to be somewhere safe from all of this trouble. Do you have a place to go?".

She wrinkles her eyes insisting with an intense tone, "I said; I will be going with my husband. As for my daughter, she will be safe here with my sister!"

I know it is not a good time to argue with her, so I smile and nod in agreement. We talk for a while until Kurt and Carlos wander downstairs from their siestas. Both of them need coffee but are eager to sit down and work out plans for the events that lay ahead.

Carlos insists with a degree of intensity, "I know a lot of hombres, senor. They can help us."

I remind him placing my coffee back on the table, "My biggest fear is a leak of information outside of this network. Anyone we bring in has to be screened to a fault. Disclosing our plans will be devastating! You can count on this government killing all of us."

He leans back against the edge of his chair, then nods, "Ok, but if we need them, I can get them."

"We are in the beginning stages of a network that can't afford mistakes! We are going up against a government that is well organized, has military superiority, and can eliminate an underground operation like ours in a heartbeat." I hesitate to make my point. "I don't know how we will screen these individuals, but I do know any mistakes will be deadly!"

The idea of this operation makes my stomach churn, but at the same time gives me a strange feeling of gratification. This is a feeling I haven't had since our involvement in the Brazilian war. We are actually making plans to go up against our government. For the next several hours, we continue our discussion regarding the people we need. Kurt brings up the very next person we definitely want to find. It's Malik Isaac, the Jamaican we served with in the navy. He will definitely be an asset. He can usually lay his hands on about anything we may need. We coordinate plans, deciding which of us will take on each responsibility.

Carlos sits back in his chair, uncomfortable due to his large build, and makes a recommendation, "Amigos, I can get twenty hombre's I trust with my life. Kurt knows at least half of them. We must have them to pull this off."

After a moment of consideration, I inject, "Kurt, help Carlos check them out. They must be loyal. Let's not take chances on any of them. They must not have a doubt regarding our plans. Don't give away any information until you both are sure they are loyal."

Kurt replies with an air of confidence, "No problem, Tony. My Navajo blood line gives me an edge when it comes to intuitions about people. Anyways, I will let them know that if they betray us, I will cut their throats and feed their families to the sharks."

I nod with a shiver. "You have the right idea. I'm going to head down to Jamaica to find Malik. I also need to find Jimmy Turner. He's the best demolition expert I know."

If my sources are correct, Malik still lives in Jamaica. It shouldn't be tough to find him. The last I heard, he is operating a cargo ship carrying legal as well as illegal shipments between ports in the Caribbean. I may even find him locked up in a jail somewhere.

Kurt brings to our attention another problem, "Hiding this sub won't be an easy task. It's going to be hard enough to steal the damn thing, much less try to hide it! How in the hell are we going to hide it in a large cavern in the middle of the Caribbean?"

I put my mind in high gear to come up with an answer to Kurt's question. It is obvious that in order to get away with such a large sub we need to disguise it. An idea suddenly manifests itself, "Yeah, that's a tough one. Satellite will pick it up in a second. Today's sophisticated radar tracking systems will also find it without a problem. I know a computer expert that works on sophisticated stealth systems. He developed most of the newest technology used today by this government. From our history together, I know he's not dedicated to this government. David Roward. If I can find him our problems will be solved. His knowledge of stealth technology is beyond what most people can even imagine. He may be able to set up Starpoint so an ocean liner can't be seen."

Kurt remains silent for a moment interpreting this information. He glances over to Carlos then back to me. He slowly begins to nod his head in acceptance, "Well…I hope you can get him then. Any system he has, had better work without fail. I don't like the idea of dying in a steel box at the bottom of the ocean."

Carlos fidgets in his chair attempting to get comfortable with his sizable frame. His bushy moustache and partial chin growth flinches with every thought he conveys. Stains from the day's perspiration show on his tan shirt. As big as he is, his facial features look rough, but in a likeable way. His hair flairs in different directions. A comb has not been near it in a while. He addresses Kurt in a bold fashion, "We have to get a close look at this submarine. There's no way we can plan to steal her without studying the area."

Kurt nods his head as if to say, 'My thoughts exactly'. He remarks, "If we work the timing just right while taking this sub, we may get away with it. Adrian and Liana should come with us. We'll look like tourists. The plan is just to take notes and decide how many men it will take to pull off this job."

Carlos injects as if the conversation is settled, "We leave in the morning amigo, if we want to get this operation started."

I felt uneasy about disrupting Carlos's business. He's been supplying drinks most of the time without collecting a tab. "Can you handle shutting the bar down for a couple of days to check out this sub?"

His bushy eyebrows raise up as his eyes focus on me. His facial expression conjures up a slight smile, "My family left me a small fortune from other businesses. This bar is just a hobby I have, amigo. I'm always looking for time to take off."

I reflect with a smile, "In that case, my bar tab will just have to disappear!" He laughs.

I have them drop me at the airport the next day on their way out of town. A search for Malik on a computer reveals him living in his homeland of Jamaica. A phone call places him in the port of Montego Bay, Jamaica, running his own cargo ship. I catch the next flight out to Jamaica on a sky jet that is known for its speed. On the way, I consider this cargo operation Malik has developed. It may just help us out with some of the odds and ends we will need.

I arrive in Montego Bay at about 10:30 in the morning having a taxi drive me down to the docks. I'm not sure how hard it's going to be to find Malik or his mystery boat. The taxi driver drives slowly along the docks in order to spot him. It's not long before I spot a radical looking ship that stands out from the rest. The colorful Jamaican artistry almost sets the water on fire. It's painted from stem to stern with colorful fish and marine life in about every color you can imagine. On the deck of the ship is the man I'm looking for, tying down his next load of cargo. I get out of the taxi and walk closer to the dock to make sure it's him. The docks are a bit run down from the obvious lack of care. The smell of fresh fish is in the air. Seagulls are busy scouring the area for a quick tidbit.

I yell out, "Is there anyone here who can get me laid Jamaican Style?"

He swings around with a look of excitement on his face and answers laughing, "Jah mon, but yah going to hab to supply de females because me be fresh out today!"

He runs across the deck, jumps to the catwalk, nearly running down a fisherman on the way and springs onto the dock. As he gets closer, his obvious grand smile beams through. Locks in his hair have gotten a bit longer since our last encounter, but it is Malik.

He runs up to me, gives me a bear hug and asks, "What brings you to paradise, mon?"

My answer is simple, "It's been too long since I've seen your ugly mug. I decided it was time to make the journey!"

He laughs in his great Jamaican style, his whole body vibrating. I have to admit that Malik is living in paradise. The ocean here is as crystal blue green as the blue eyes of a beautiful woman. The air is clean like taking a deep breath of sunshine. Asking Malik to leave here is going to be a difficult task. The only convincing debate is that the island I call Starpoint is just as magnificent.

We board his ship by way of a gangplank that creaks as we walk across it. The ocean along with the weather has weakened it over the years. The ship looks solid enough, but the colorful artwork is a sight to behold. I'm not sure how much cargo he has been hauling. The ship's paint job must have taken him time to complete.

I look over the vessel, taking in the complexity of the artwork. "How are you doing these days? Is the freight business keeping you busy?"

He confesses, "Me do fine Tony, but me don't get good help here. You come to Jamaica to be me second mate or just to see me ugly mug?"

I have to give him the run down, especially before he decides to make me the captain. "Let's sit down with a cold drink, and I'll fill you in."

We enter the boat's cabin which contains more graffiti. I begin to fill him in on all the details, including his importance to the operation. I give him as much information as I can in the brief amount of time I have.

He listens with a puzzled look on his face until he interrupts, "You know me help yah outwit dis, but if me stop moving cargo, me lose me ship. All me money is here mon, in this ship!"

"Malik, I would never ask you to give your ship up, in fact we can really use it to move cargo to the island. How much do you owe on her?"

He quickly answers calculating the amount in his head, "About two-hundred-and-sixty-five-thousand dollars, mon!"

My intuition tells me Malik will help us if I get him out of debt with the ship. I smile and wink, conveying to him, "I know someone that just may help you pay off your ship if you can help."

He smiles from ear to ear and bellows, "If you can do dat mon, den the boat and me be yours! Just promise me mon; you do not joke with me now."

I figure between the money I have been saving and with Carlos's help, we can pay the boat off or at least pay a good deal of it down to buy us some time. What good was money anyway, if you couldn't spend it?

I have one more question, "Just how good does this ship run?"

He hesitates before answering, "It mostly runs really smooth, just some small problems with de engine. De paint job be alright."

It's not the answer I'm hoping for, but one I'm expecting. I suppose I'll spend the next few days doing maintenance on his ship. It has to be ready for any voyage. As the day continues, I give Malik a list of items we need to restructure Starpoint. He looks over the list, acknowledging a few items he can get.

It is important to get everything on this list, so I ask him, "I really need you to pull together everything together I have written down. If you can't find new items, then anything used will have to do. These are important or our operation will fall apart."

He looks at me with his usual big smile, "If yah need dese things, den me do my best to get them."

Sounds just like the old Malik I knew in the navy. As we work away on the engine, a news bulletin interrupts the music on the radio. The reporter declares, "The United Nations Government is calling for the first lottery to be held on September 25th."

A panicky feeling comes over me, one that will not go away quickly. All the work we have to do to prepare for our underground retaliation against is going to be extremely difficult. We have to put things in high gear; there is no time to waste. Many people's lives depend upon stopping this lottery. It's just over five months from today.

The reporter continues, "Rioting is continuing to escalate in all parts of the world. Military police have been called out in massive numbers to counter the violence. In Spain today, U.N. military police returned fire when a group of citizens threw stones chanting anti-government criticisms. Twenty-three were killed as the riot grew more intense. Lottery committee officials remain steadfast in their convictions to proceed with these plans. The first lottery is set to be held on September 25th of this year."

We spend two days going through the ship, making sure it is fully seaworthy. I am not sure if the paint job will be a hindrance or a benefit. At sea it will definitely stand out, but it won't register a threat. A government vessel might ignore it. I just don't have the guts to tell Malik he needs to repaint it. Besides, it is actually beginning to grow on me.

Three days pass, and I leave Jamaica having finished the repairs. I relinquish to Malik the job of gathering the supplies. I know if anyone can gather these items together, Malik can. It's important that I get back to Mexico. Kurt and Carlos should have returned following inspection of the sub. Everything has to fall into place in order for our operation to succeed. I just hope we can gather the proper people together in time.

I arrive in Cancun and make my way to the Casa' de la Parrot. Kurt and Carlos are sitting at a table towards the back of the bar having a discussion. I'm just hopeful it is a positive one. We conclude our normal greetings, as I try to read the expressions on their faces. They look as if things are tolerable, but I just need to hear it for myself.

Kurt clears his throat. "This sub is just what we need, but it's well guarded. We're going to need at least twenty well trained men to get this metal monster to Starpoint."

Carlos takes a solid shot of his drink, some liquor trickles down his mustache, then he adds, "Amigo. The best time to ambush it is a Saturday night or early Sunday morning. Only a few men will be guarding it."

Kurt injects into the conversation, "Once out of port, we need to make a tactful run for the sea or we will surely end up in a watery grave! If your friend Steve can devise a stealth camouflage from the moment we take her, then we may just be able to get away."

Carlos nods in agreement. He fumbles with his glass that no longer contains any liqueur. He contemplates his need for another drink.

I consider the information for a second, then add, "I want the guards darted with a five-hour knockout drug. We don't want blood on our hands. We all need to agree on this; if blood is to be spilled, it won't be from our hands."

We have a few drinks to toast the success of the operation, then Kurt decides to ask the big question, "How did everything turn out with Malik, Tony?"

I raise my eyebrows, answering, "Malik just does not want anything to do with us!"

They look at each other with a puzzled expression.

I add, "I can't figure out why he won't help!" I let them wonder for a moment before I give in and supply them the good news. I crack a smile indicating my bullshit, injecting, "Pay backs are hell! Of course Malik is in with us; I wouldn't have left there until he was!"

They both glare at me as if they are looking down the barrels of Winchester's.

I feel a bit uncomfortable, quickly adding, "The best news partners, he has a cargo ship large enough to carry all the supplies we need to Starpoint. We only need to pay it off to get him on his way."

Both of them look at me with mistrust but nod in acceptance. It's a brilliant way to get the details of the ship purchase out of the way. It's just not the right time to tell them about the paint job. Why spoil the day?

The next few days go by quickly, attempting to reach the people we have in mind. I locate Jimmy Turner, the explosives expert, in Australia working with a mining operation. He agrees to fly to Cancun as quickly as possible. I have to coax him with nonsense. His company is taking a break from its operations.

Steve Roward, the stealth expert, is harder to track down. It takes twenty phone calls to locate him in Italy. Apparently, he's doing private research for a company there, but is willing to take a few days off to visit me in Cancun. Carlos and Kurt locate quite a few other people with various backgrounds they trust to join us for a reunion.

Kurt knows a retired submarine captain that quit the New World Navy over hatred of its values. His name is Captain Kyle "Bud" Butler, and he has years of extensive submarine duty. This man will be a jewel to complement our ever growing network of people.

By the end of three days, we have tracked down and sent for seventy-three people that hopefully will join our delicate operation and help change the world. We've handpicked each and every one for their knowledge, expertise, dependability, and honesty. I just hope we picked correctly.

Most of them are on their way to Cancun or due to arrive within the next three days. Carlos makes arrangements to get an old movie theater to hold a meeting in. Keeping everything secretive is difficult but absolutely necessary. We tell everyone as little as possible, thus limiting information leaks. Mostly we tell them it is a reunion of sorts. Individuals begin to arrive from all parts of the globe. Men and women, sixty-three of them, from all ethnic origins and backgrounds are arriving to get the jist of what is going on. Rumors have everyone guessing as to the purpose of the large gathering. We keep everything low-key so as not to create problems.

The first person I need to speak with privately is Steve Roward, the stealth system expert. I need to get him working on the stealth systems as quickly as possible. He arrives just as he said, and it's great to see him once again. His clean, tailored clothing is a welcome change from what I have been used to. His hair is neatly trimmed with a clean-shaven face. I sit down with him in a private area and begin to educate him on our plans describing the island, the cavern, and the purpose they will serve. His excitement is electrifying! He knows just the systems we will be need and how to get them quickly. He also has a great system for the submarine, one that he just updated.

He informs me, "This system will read the surrounding waters signature, duplicate it, and add it to the signature of the submarine. This sub will now give off a radar signature that is just like the water surrounding it. The submarine will completely disappear on radar, satellite, or any sonar tracking devices. It's really a marvel we just finished developing. The beautiful thing is no one has any information about it. The system is small, self-contained, and easily transported. It can be up and running in a matter of minutes if I prepare it properly. It will truly become a stealth submarine!"

He thinks for a second, then continues to ramble in his excitement. "Now the island with its cavern will be a little more complex. A system will have to be implemented that will read the ever-changing island and replicate these signatures bit by bit." He hesitates for a second, "This system will then piece the bits together into a sequential mapping of the island. The signatures will be disbursed as a map, giving the island the illusion that nothing is below it or within it except for the normal structures. Any objects within the cavern or caves will be hidden from radar, sonar, and satellite tracking. As long as the system is running, it will hide everything!"

I try to follow the information as he delves deeper into the subject matter, but his intelligence is beyond what I can relate to.

Steve continues, "It will take two weeks to set the island up properly and will require generators to keep it running. The equipment I need has to be readily available." He is as excited beyond words and ready to get to work immediately. I get Steve into a room and allow him to start working on his quick drafts.

The next person I need to speak with privately is Jimmy Turner, the explosive expert. He arrives hours after Steve, and of course our greetings are stupendous. Jim is a man that has remained in tip top shape. His muscular frame along with his obvious workout regimen is demonstrated as he grips my hand in what seems like a death grip. I slide my hand from his in order to get the feeling back. Pulling Jimmy aside, I go over the entire plans with him. He demonstrates the same enthusiasm.

"Opening up the cavern entrance without causing structural damage will be no problem. I'll have to survey the island, cavern, and entrance, but I don't see a problem with altering it. I already have access to the explosives and detonators."

"Good, then I can count on you?"

"Of course! It'll just be something new I can blow up, a new challenge of sorts," he says gripping my hand again, causing near paralysis.

The main meeting is about to be begin. Everyone's enthusiasm is upbeat, making the effort much more gratifying. Most everyone has arrived, so anyone arriving late will have to be given details later.

I start the meeting off by describing the situation, giving details of our operation, and describing how our plans will be implemented. Kurt and Carlos fill in details about the submarine and its usefulness to our operation. They describe how its main purpose will be to evacuate as many people as we can from a chosen grid area before the poisonous gases are released. We know we cannot save everyone, but we will try to rescue as many people as possible.

The meeting begins to remind me of an old-time revival meeting. The longer we discuss these future plans, the more excited everyone becomes. Some individuals recommend bringing other people into the operation. We totally dismiss this concept, reminding them they have been carefully chosen individually. We need to have a totally confidential group, without leakage for this operation to occur. It is absolutely necessary that no one discuss this operation with anyone outside of the people directly involved. The first meeting flows flawlessly; our plans are totally underway.

Kurt, Carlos, Steve, and I decide that the information regarding the stealth systems will be only known by the four of us. It is the only way to keep the operation safe, giving it a much better chance of success.

Some of the people decide to stay and get started immediately, while others have to return to their homes before they can devote time to the operation. They have to make new arrangements in their lives in order to join this operation.

I think we have reached a point with this organization that calls for a bit of a celebration. Carlos opens the bar up for all of us to celebrate. He even gets a Jamaican 'Bob Marley' style band to entertain us. It is his idea to kick the celebration off with the right theme. Today we made decisions that will affect us for the rest of our lives.

There is a ravishing woman that I have had an eye on since I arrived here. My love life has practically been on hold for a while now and tonight will be a good time to change that. I have been on the move so much that a real relationship has never worked out for me, although I have known many fine women in my life.

The celebration gets off to a great start. We all need something to feel good about since the announcement of this lottery. I spot the same beautiful senorita and decide to approach her with as much charm as I can muster up. As I walked over to her, I notice she has blue eyes as beautiful as finely polished gemstones.

Her long shimmering black hair glistens from the sparkling bar lights as if her hair has lights of its own. As I approach her, I am again spellbound by her natural beauty. Her complexion is soft and clean with a beautiful light brown tone. She has a pleasant gusty laugh that clings in the air. Usually, I have a great line to start things off with, but my mind is blank! I decide to be honest and just say what is on my mind.

I blurt out, "You are the most beautiful woman I have ever seen. I just have to get you into my life!" I could kick myself for using such a lame pick up line.

She sighs and looks at me with a slight smile on her face. I am sure that I have blown my first approach and am not sure what to do next. She winks, takes my right arm in hers, and leads me to the dance floor. I could feel her body shudder involuntarily as I touch her back. She looks at me and whispers, "Now that you have me in your life, do you know how to handle me?"

Sometimes it just pays to be lame! From the moment we start to converse, it just seems like we belong together. The longer I'm in her company, the more infatuated I become. She is able to stir up feelings within me that I had forgotten. I can't remember feeling this way so quickly about a woman in any of my prior relationships.

She indulges me, "My name is Catalina Delray. I'm originally from Spain, but I had to move here to Mexico because of world politics." She rests her hand lightly on the back of my neck. She continues, "Spain has been a risky place to live. A few years ago, it attempted to pull away from the United Nations. My father was a general with the Spanish army and instrumental in the attempt to pull Spain away. We left in fear of military retaliation. Since our move, most of my fears of reprisals have subsided. My father attempts to stays out of mainstream politics."

I answer, "I have a real problem with the U.N. myself. I would like to meet your father. How is your family adjusting?"

She nods with a slight smile, "Let's go where we can be alone. There are things I can't keep bottled up inside."

When the time is right, I lead Catalina to the room I'm staying in, above the bar. Her smile lights the room up the way sunshine lights up the day. We kiss softly and tenderly while my heart begins to pound. She commences to unsnap my belt buckle as our kisses become more passionate. Her blouse is wrapped loosely around her breasts, tied like a scarf. I can feel her heart beating faster as I pull her chest close to mine. Unsnapping her blouse, she slowly arches backwards, breathing heavily in anticipation. My heart is pounding out of my chest as she unsnaps her skirt, dropping it to the floor. I gaze into her eyes. Our bodies meet, giving me the sensation our very souls have been entwined. We make love for hours. She is not like any woman I have slept with before. The passion between us is indescribable; she ignites my soul! We spend hours caressing one another as we slowly fall into a restful sleep.

I wake next to her feeling like the ground has shaken under me. She remains sleeping, so I lay beside her for a good twenty minutes just watching her sleep. No other woman has bewitched me the way she has. I am truly feeling possessed! I kiss her softly as she awakens, and her smile just melts me away. If I'm going to include her in my life, I will need to include her in our plans. For now, I honor my agreement to be silent.

She rolls towards me with a delicate stretch and a smile. "I have to check in with my family. Can we meet later?"

My mind is still in a whirl. I answer, "I wish you could just stay here with me all day, but I have to get some work done. Let's meet tonight about six."

We kiss and she quietly leaves with a wink. After taking a quick shower, I walk down to the first floor and meet Kurt at the bottom step.

He winks approvingly, saying, "You certainly know how to pick your women!"

I smile, replying, "This one may just be around for a while!"

He laughs, reflecting on my past. I have never stayed with one girl for very long, but I think I may just prove him wrong for once.

Kurt reminds me, "Don't forget, Kyle Butler, the retired submarine captain, is going to arrive today at noon. We need to sit down with him privately and persuade him to join our troops. We need a man like this to help us operate this sub. Hopefully, he will take the responsibility as our captain."

"Consider me there. I'll put my best game face on."

Kurt makes another fact known, "Steve Rowland and two other individuals flew out early this morning to gather the stealth systems. He said he will gather whatever is needed and return before we leave for the cavern."

It's necessary that everything arrive in Jamaica simultaneously when we're ready to leave. The stealth systems have to be kept a secret from most everyone involved. Steve insists that rustling them will be a piece of cake. He's not normally a thief by nature, but under these circumstances people's lives depend upon it.

The timing of this operation is crucial. Having the cavern, set up properly in time to steal the sub is a must. Everything has to be completed quickly before the government announces the grid selection of the first lottery. We have to be ready to move by the time, they make this announcement. It's the only way we can get as many people out of harm's way as possible.

Our first task is to get supplies to the cavern as quickly as possible. A list of supplies has to be finalized and gathered to load on the boat in Jamaica. The items Malik is accumulating will only get us started. Items such as scuba gear, welding equipment, steel supports, air compressors, electrical generators, wiring, three small boats, food, water, and even underwater scooters are on his list. We still need quite a few other items. I plan to contact Malik today to find out how he is doing.

I spend a few hours in a room compiling information sources on equipment we need. My mind isn't completely tuned in to the task at hand. I keep thinking of Catalina. She is probably the best thing that has happened to me in a long time. I do my best to finish up the list. It's going to be difficult to find all the items we need.

Kurt enters the room, along with a gentleman I have never seen before. He is somewhat distinguished, with a clean-cut white beard, looking much like the typical sea captain.

Kurt introduces him. "Tony, I want you to meet Kyle Butler, better known as 'Bud' Butler."

I hold out my hand, saying, "I hope what we have to tell you will sit well with you and maybe even get your involvement."

He slightly smiles, nods, and then sits down ready to hear what we have to say. We spend the next hour explaining the details of the operation we have planned, especially the need for the submarine. He listens, extremely alert, nodding every so often to our presentation. I'm not sure how he is accepting all of it. He retains a great poker face.

Finally, out of nervousness, I ask the question, "Do you think you can help us?"

He sighs, leans back in his chair, takes a breath, and says, "I will only help you if you follow my advice. Allow me to include a few submarine specialists I know. If you follow my advice, we may just accomplish your mission."

I feel the weight of several hundred pounds lift off my shoulders.

Kurt asks, "What kind of advice do you plan to ask for?"

I quickly speak, "It doesn't matter Kurt; we have him on board!" My mouth speaks a bit faster than my brain.

Kyle answers with a forgiving glance in my direction, "Just listen to my recommendations and let me control the sub."

"It's totally agreeable with me!" We shake hands, as I excuse myself to get a drink from Carlos. I really need it!

The next few days go by very quickly. I contact Malik to make sure he is gathering all the supplies and hardware together in time for our arrival. He informs me that only a few items are giving him trouble, but that he may have them in time for us to leave for Starpoint. Carlos and I scrounge together enough money to pay down the cargo ship, along with most of the supplies we have already gathered. With this news, Malik becomes more energetic than ever in regard to finding all of the items. It takes another day to gather up the equipment and begin packing for the trip to Jamaica. Steve shows up with the stealth systems for both the submarine and the cavern.

I meet Steve at the freight terminal inside the airport. His expression has the usual flare. A large case in his right hand indicates he at least has part of the system.

"Hey partner, how did you make out with the items we need?"

He answers, "Taking the systems was easier than inventing them. I managed to get everything I need. I used another person's security pass to enter the building that housed the equipment. It won't be missed for a while. I recorded all of it as being shipped to another facility."

"You're the man. Let's get these crates loaded up and get them shipped to Jamaica."

We carefully conceal the equipment in crates. We camouflage the supplies and ship them out to Malik. It's finally time to pack up our own belongings, and head to Malik's cargo ship. We drive back to Carlos's bar to make the final preparations for our voyage. Most everyone is already preparing for the trip.

Catalina and I are becoming very close. The more time I spend with her, the more infatuated I become. She is totally committed to our operation, suggesting that her father may be able to help if it becomes necessary.

Catalina insists, "I'm not going to let you go without me!"

"It's just too dangerous. I don't know what problems we may encounter," I insist, making my best effort to persuade her.

She gives me her saddest expression. "Listen. I can help cook, and I've had experience scuba diving. You've got to let me come with you!"

"Ok," I answer reluctantly, "But as soon as we finish the cavern, you're going back to Cancun where you'll be safe. I'm making sure that all the women will be going back"

She smiles and laughs, giving me a huge passionate kiss. I just hope I'm not making a big mistake.

CHAPTER 4

CAVERN STARPOINT

Today, Jamaica is on my mind. All the equipment is packed and on its way to Montego Bay. Fifty-two of us are making the trip to the cavern, Starpoint. Twenty-five will take the ninety-six-foot cargo ship, while the others will meet at a pre-determined place near the actual cavern. We do not want to draw attention to ourselves, so we take separate flights. Groups of four to five people will travel together, just to keep any suspicion to a minimum. A large group traveling from Mexico to Jamaica may not seem suspicious, but we did not want to take any chances. Carlos and several others stay in Mexico just to keep the bar open, giving the impression that everything is normal. Carlos, along with Kyle Butler, will take charge of the submarine operation when the time is right.

Kurt pleads to Adrian and Liana as a last-minute effort, "You girls need to stay in Mexico. This trip is going to be too dangerous and risky. Liana really needs to keep up with her studies."

Liana remarks with a spiteful attitude, "If you are going to leave me behind, I will just follow you on my own. I have money to get there without a problem."

I believe she will do just that. It is a battle that Kurt will lose in the long run. Kurt finally agrees. "When the time comes to bring the submarine to the island, then all you girls will fly back home. By that time most of the cavern should be finished, and our operation will really become dangerous."

"We promise to leave then; just give us an opportunity to help out," Liana said as she tweaks Kurt's cheek.

Kurt barks another order in an attempt to save face, "Fine, but remember it's only a temporary situation."

Kurt, Adrian, Liana, Catalina, and I board a plane together in Cancun, flying directly to Jamaica. The flight is smooth and quick. Malik is waiting for us at the baggage claim area, standing there with a large grin on his face.

He remarks, "Dis be da best looking group dat come off de plane so far. Only yah should see some of de ones before yah."

Kurt had not seen Malik since they served together in the navy, so it's time for a great reunion.

Kurt answers with a normal sarcastic comment: "Malik, if you get any uglier, we'll have to use you as the anchor. What have you been doing all these years?"

"Jah mon, but the women, dey still want me! Just kicking back mon under the Jamaican sun."

Catalina, Liana, and Adrian get a kick out of Malik and his unique Jamaican style. They have never met anyone as colorful as Malik. He does have a way with the ladies.

Following several minutes of introductions, we climb into Malik's vehicle and head down to the docks. Kurt has not seen the cargo ship, and I haven't told him about the unique paint job. He will see it for himself soon enough, and I can only guess what his reaction will be like.

We pull up to the cargo ship and get out of the vehicle. I can tell by the expression on Kurt's face we are about to have a scene.

Kurt barks, "Amigo! What on earth is this painted up for?"

Malik twists his head and answers with a sparkle of confidence in his voice, "It's the pride of the fleet, mon!"

Deep down I'm laughing my ass off, but I have to keep my composure.

I quickly remark to help save the situation, "It's going to be great camouflage, and it shouldn't draw any attention."

Kurt looks at me like I am crazy, answering, "Get attention! How in the hell could it not get attention? It looks like a zoo on water!"

The laughter is about to roll out of me, but somehow I manage to keep it inside. I look at the girls; all three are smirking doing their best not to laugh out loud.

Catalina attempts to help the situation. "I think it's very attractive, sort of like a party boat."

Of course this gives Malik a great boost of recognition. It's just the kind of comment he needs to boast more about his ship.

Malik remarks, "Thank you, me ship has to have Jamaican style!"

Kurt rolls his eyes and shakes his head from side to side, answering, "Well, let's make the best of it. I hope it runs."

"We worked on it for two-and-a-half days. It runs like a fine-tuned sports car," I add. "Anyways, it's all we got."

"Well let's get this puppy on the water then. Times a wasting," Kurt finally remarks, shaking his head back and forth even more.

Within two hours, everyone has arrived, totaling all twenty-five. All the equipment is checked out, including the supplies that arrive late. Everything is secured and strapped down for the voyage ahead of us. Steve Roward has all of his equipment with him in crates.

It is a great day in Jamaica, with a cool breeze blowing from the east. Malik cranks up the ship's diesels, and a few of us pull the ropes in from the dock. We are finally on our way, with our destiny in our own hands. The day is starting out perfectly. The ship runs very smoothly, especially after all the work Malik and I accomplished. The ocean is magnificent, and three dolphins give us an escort out to sea. The day is still early, and the weather can't be better.

Malik named the ship 'Sea Jewel' because it reminds him of the jewel of the sea. The cargo ship is ninety-six feet long, with a twenty-two foot beam, and an eleven-foot draft. The fuel capacity is two-thousand-five-hundred gallons, but a short trip like this will not consume much fuel. It won't take more than one-and-a-half days to get to Starpoint.

Once we arrive on the main island, we have to unload the supplies and equipment into smaller boats in order to get everything ashore. We plan to sleep in tents until we move into the cavern below. A type of staging area will be setup on the flat natural area of the cavern to keep everything organized. Generators are going to be used to give the whole cavern power and light. Getting them into the cavern is going to be a job in itself. The fumes from the generator will have to be siphoned out through exhaust fans. All these things need to be finished quickly.

Our first order of business is to get Jimmy Turner working on the cavern opening, in order to fit the submarine into the cavern. He has to carefully set explosives that should open the entrance without losing any structure to the cavern.

Jim reassured me before we left Cancun. "Setting these explosives will be a simple matter. Just leave it to me, and you will have an entrance to this cavern that will astound you." He will meet us at a predetermined area near the island—with all the necessary explosives in hand.

I also need Steve Roward to begin working on the stealth system for the cavern. We need to get this system up and working quickly to keep any activity off radar scopes or satellite scans.

Malik, in a quick motioning gesture, directs me to the stern of the ship. He is anxious to show me a few extra items that he was able to get his hands on. He pulls a large cover, exposing a small, two-man submarine about sixteen feet in length.

"Partner, how in the world did you get your hands on this?" I exclaim with a bit of shock from the sight. "This will definitely help with the underwater work we need to do."

"Jah mon, me do my best for you."

The next item seems to give Malik a bit more excitement. He exposes a large outdoor grill setup smiling like he's about to win an award. I pat him on the back and acknowledge. "You're a fine man; you really outdid yourself."

It is true: Malik has pulled together a lot of complicated equipment in a short period of time. I can always count on him in a pinch. He exclaims, "The grill is Me best gift to yah mon. It keep us eating mon, even if everything be bloodfire." "We scraped together all the food we could locate, let's just hope the fish are as numerous as I remember at the island. It's hard to gather enough food when its in such short supply."

Malik and I spend several hours looking over the items he has gathered. The skip boats were military surplus, but in good shape all the same. The two-man submarine is also used and in need of some repair, although it appears like it should be easy to fix. With everything considered, we have enough equipment to get a good start on the island. Kurt remains busy sorting the inventory in preparation to unload equipment. Catalina, Adrian, and Liana are having a great time making preparations for the first meal of the day.

I just have to go to the bow of the ship and take a large breath of fresh air. It's great to see the whole operation going so smoothly. I gaze out on the ocean, savoring how the sea always has me bewitched. To me, the ocean is an incredible world of its own, one that I can never get enough of. The early evening is displaying a sunset that is bizarre beyond words. The setting sun gives the sky a pageantry of neon colors that fade as the sun sluggishly disappears. I have to savor the moment. The sunset is always too eager.

The girls fix a reasonable dinner, allowing everyone on board to eat only minimum portions. Our food has to last until we know what the future has in store. Kurt breaks out a small crate of rum, taking one bottle out of its contents. He opens the bottle and passes it around to celebrate the first of many nights.

"Tonight, we celebrate. The days ahead may not be as good as this day is," Kurt toasts with a confident smile on his face.

"Partner, pass that bottle over. I'm in one of those rare moods." I wink at Catalina as the ship sways from the breaking waves against the hull.

The night passes as we discuss the upcoming events that can make or break our operation. I am in awe that everything is going according to plan. Eventually, most of us find our sleeping areas for the night. A few stay awake and alert, steering the ship towards Starpoint.

The morning breaks through the night, with a sunrise as awesome as the sunset. That great Caribbean breeze blows across the deck, giving the day one beautiful start. We are making great time as the ship plunges across the ocean. Catalina wakes me up with a sexual gesture that makes my spine tingle. I respond to her foreplay with pure loving desire. She fills in the missing voids that lack in past relationships. People on board are beginning to stir, so we hurry our romantic interlude. So much for a long romantic morning.

The day gets underway, and we work on various types of equipment, making sure everything works properly. We assemble the generators, check the scuba gear, and take a complete inventory of everything we have. The used scuba gear Malik has gathered is in fairly good condition. He even remembered to bring aboard a compressor to refill the tanks as the need arises. We check out twenty tanks allowing anywhere from ten to twenty divers underwater at the same time. The debris remaining after blasting will require a large group of divers. Nothing can be overlooked as we get closer to the island.

Malik gives a blast of the fog horns, as we approach a familiar island. I can see a few people along the shore line waving a red flag. We have arrived at the check point. Jim Turner and the rest of the devotees signal us as instructed. They flash us twice, hesitate, and then flash us twice more with a strobe light. Kurt and I launch two of the skip boats. We steadily speed toward shore watching the group gather at our approach.

Kurt yells as we approach the shore, "Get everybody ready. We're not wasting time on drifters."

I notice more luggage on the shore than I think we can carry, "If we can't get everything loaded, then it's going to remain here on this island."

We get to shore and all twenty-seven people gather near the boats to load up. Jim has his explosives packed in sealed containers. I survey the items piled on the shore, "Start loading evenly or we may capsize these boats before we ever make it to the Sea Jewel. It's a long way to swim."

We load everyone with care along with the equipment and return back to the ship. The skip boats handle the weight with precision even with the slight chop of the surf. The containers are handled carefully with concerns about the explosive contents.

Jim instructs as each one is moved, "Don't shake them up if you want to see tomorrow. I'll guarantee it will be the last mistake you'll make."

Caution takes hold as each container is moved onto the ship with extreme care. The last of the containers is stowed aboard as the skip boats get pulled from the water.

I extend my hand to Jim, "Welcome, partner. Glad to see you made it ok."

Jim gives me a firm grip returning my greeting, "You got a loud ship here. Did you borrow this from a local circus?"

"It's a long story, just be glad we have a ship to use."

I announce to everyone, "It's time to head to our final destination. The cavern is within two hours of our present location. In order to speed up the unloading process, everything of necessity, needs to be placed near the crane. All items such as tents, food, generators, and scuba equipment will be the first items we will need to unload."

Malik sounds the fog horn for a second time as we round the edge of the present island. A direct course to our final destination is plotted. My orders are followed as everyone helps with the equipment. The Sea Jewel gathers speed as we race along in the Carribean Sea. From the bow of the ship, I watch the waves in the distance enjoying the beauty of the crystal waters.

The area I have named Starpoint appears ahead, looking just as magnificent as I remembered. The large, crystal clear lagoon can be seen, and waves splash against the surrounding rocks in a rhythmic pattern. The island itself contains a sharp, rising, mountainous terrain with jungle vegetation surrounding it. Volcanic action must have pushed this island up from the sea millions of years ago. The bulk of the cavern is within this sharply rising mountain that lay before us. The marine life on this island remains abundant and will keep all of us well fed as long as we remain.

Malik steers the ship into a position that allows us to easily unload the equipment and supplies onto the smaller boats. We anchor the ship and begin the tedious chore of unloading. The size of the lagoon makes it easy to get fairly close, and the process of unloading the essential equipment begins. The crane lifts crates of equipment, lowering them carefully onto the boats.

Kurt sets out on foot to find an area to set up camp. He finds an area on the island near the lagoon. It will make a perfect camp. It's hidden from the shore line but close enough to the cavern to get our work done. Looking into the lagoon from the edge of the shore, we can see the entrance to the underwater cavern about ninety-five feet down. The water is so crystal clear that the entrance looks like a dark hole in the coral reef. The depth of the lagoon remains just as deep as it flows out toward the ocean, making it a great entrance for the sub. Opening the cavern will be our only problem, but hopefully Jim's explosive charges will rectify that.

With most of the equipment on shore, everyone pitches in to set up camp included the tents and screen rooms. Kurt and a few people finish the generator assembly, extending electrical lines for a constant flow of electricity and light. The whole camp is beginning to shape up fairly quickly. A larger tent is erected for a dining area, allowing us to escape the insects on the island. Everyone remains busy at camp while Jim Turner and I decide to investigate the cavern. I'm eager to let Jim see the entrance for himself.

Jim explains the process, "These explosions will mostly blow outward, still keeping the integrity of the cavern intact. All we need to do is remove the debris, until the opening is large enough to allow the submarine to enter. We can do this in stages."

"I hope we can get this done in record time partner," I remark recalling the time table we are under.

"We'll just have to work day and night until we have it done," Jim replies.

We decide to make one dive before dusk, and we don our scuba gear entering the crystal clear water. We make a steady descent towards the cavern entrance, noticing large schools of yellow tangs flickering around the coral heads. Slightly off to our right, a large manta ray is making its rounds, gliding through the water. We approach the cavern entrance that contains a large gaping cave leading back into a dark abyss. The circumference of this opening has to be at least eighteen to twenty feet around. Jim points toward areas that has be removed to allow for an even a larger opening.

He writes on a slate, 'These areas will be easy to remove; removing debris will be a job.' I give Jim the typical thumbs up to indicate my approval.

We enter the cave, shining our lights into the ever-darkening entrance. The cavern opens gradually becoming larger as we follow it inward. Suddenly, my flashlight catches the form of a ten foot tiger shark heading our way. I nudge Jim, signaling him to move to the side to give the shark a wide thoroughfare. We move aside as the large sea creature swims by us, taking his fair share of the room. The shark glides by like our presence there meant nothing. His jagged teeth show in the dim light. A shudder runs up my spine as I watch in awe. We move forward for about another thirty feet, and the entrance opens up before us. Ahead is an enormous cavern that flows without end. I signal Jim to head for the surface. Both of us bob to the surface, while Jim looks around in awe.

The only words he manages to exclaim looking around is, "This is magnificent!"

Our flashlights shine around exposing parts of the interior. The ceiling reaches a height of about ninety feet above the water line, while the sides are easily four-hundred feet wide. The length of the cavern is even longer as we try to visualize the end our flashlight beams don't reach. To our left is the flat landing area I remember and described to Jim earlier. It's large enough for a hefty camp to be set up. Several caves run off in various directions giving it an even bigger zone. It's a perfect hidden base with enormous potential.

I determine that, utilizing waterproof containers, we can bring down some of the equipment with less effort. The small sub can carry larger items that have to remain dry. We look around for a few more minutes before deciding to head back. Jim and I swim back to the lagoon as we follow the same path.

Climbing out of the water, Jim remarks with conviction, "When you described this cavern, I admit, I was a bit skeptical. Now that I have seen it for myself, I can't believe how incredible it really is!"

"It's going to be perfect for our purposes, and will keep us hidden away from the military. The sub should be well hidden in there," I am relieved it has remained intact after all these years.

We talk at length about the explosives. Jim reflects how easily they can be placed for maximum effectiveness. He reviews his general plan, "The structure of the cavern is plenty sound enough to handle the detonations. The water should act as a shock absorber when the explosions occur. Each blast shouldn't have any effect on the structure."

"You're the man in charge of this operation. I know we can count on you partner."

We return to camp just in time for the evening meal. The crew has finished setting up all the tents, making the camp look like a small village. Kurt points towards a tent set up for Catalina and me. "You can warm it up any time now amigo," he remarks smugly.

"Thanks, I believe it will get warmed up soon enough."

I set myself down by the fire for a few minutes when I hear a petrifying scream! It sounds just like Catalina and is coming from our tent. I jump up quickly as Catalina lunges from the opening.

She screams, "Snakes!"

I grab a long stick, and head into the tent to rescue her from these slithering menaces. Catalina is pointing frantically into the tent yelling, "There's at least four or five of them in there!"

I carefully enter the tent, noticing at least three snakes, two of them in coiled positions. I carefully poke at one of them, but it doesn't move. Kurt comes running over with and a few other people curious about the activity. I press the stick against the snake even harder, without a hint of movement. Looking closer at the snakes, I realize they are made of rubber. The first person that comes to my mind is Malik. He's up to his old practical jokes again. I grab one of the snakes and bring it outside. The rubber snake looks surprisingly real even in the light. I can hear Malik snickering in the his tent. The look on Catalina's face as we stand looking at the snakes is worth a million dollars.

I explain to her. "Malik loves his practical jokes, even though they get out of hand."

She cracks a smile and suggests, "I will definitely get even with him for this! If it's the last thing I do."

Malik comes out of his tent grinning, but apologetic to Catalina, "Me give you my word as a Jamaican, dat you not be de target of me joke. I try to joke Tony, but you walk into de tent instead."

Catalina remarks with a stern flavor to her voice, "I might forgive you; just get ready for one of my jokes. I may not be as nice."

C H A P T E R 5

THE DEMOLITION

As morning begins, all of us wake up early to get a good start on the day. I lift back the flap of the tent as the sun projects its rays on my face. A morning dampness hangs in the air. The camp is situated so a view of the ocean can be seen through the vegetation. It looks like it's going to be a promising day.

Jim approaches me in an eager state. He has drawn up plans showing how the explosives will be placed. "The first round of explosives should remove most of the opening, taking out sections of rock that project outward. I will adjust each charge accordingly, so the maximum effect will remove the greatest sections of rock. Each explosive will impact the rock, not the structure of the cavern."

I reply, trying to cover a yawn, "Then comes the hard work, partner. We have to remove the loose rock underwater, and mostly by hand."

Kurt walks up hearing the conversation. He jokes, "Yeah Tony, I always thought some of your rocks were loose."

"Well, they just keep getting looser by the minute," I answer as I pour myself a cup of coffee.

"Sounds like a good plan, brother. Just make sure we only have to set the charges once." Kurt's humor takes some pressure off our shoulders. The task ahead of us is not going to be easy. Working underwater to remove debris is a dangerous undertaking.

While Jim is preparing for the first detonation, Steve Roward begins the task of compiling his stealth equipment. He connects his hardware to our power source and begins the tedious job of programming his computers. He'll gather readings from all over the island in an attempt to render a computer duplicate of the island. All this information will be necessary including tide and weather changes. He will slowly compile a map of the island, which will be utilized to open up his stealth software. Steve takes a few people and begins gathering the information he will need.

Malik and the girls gather together the scuba equipment for our first dive. Jim, Kurt, and I plan to make the dive to set the first round of explosives in the appropriate locations. A few others stand by with scuba gear, just in case there's an accident.

Jim gathers the plastic explosives and connects the electrical wires to each charge, making sure each is in an appropriate order. The main cable from the explosives will run to the surface and then connect to a control box. The charges should be synchronized as they detonate for maximum effect. If everything proceeds correctly, the largest sections of the cavern entrance will be eliminated. We will dive down and inspect the damage. If everything appears safe, we will begin the debris removal operation.

Twelve divers will work in teams taking sections of loose rock and coral out of the way. A cable running from the ships crane will help pull the largest rock debris from the entrance. Cleanup should be the most tedious and dangerous part of this job.

Jim has all eight explosives wired, so it's time to get wet. The three of us put on our dive gear and get into the lagoon. The water has not changed a bit from the old days. The clarity is almost as good as it gets. The rocks around us catch an occasional wave as we enter.

Jim instructs us before placing the regulator in his mouth, "Follow my lead as we descend. I'll signal where each explosive should go. Ready?"

"I've got your back, partner," I respond, inflating my buoyancy compensator slightly.

Malik hands us the explosives, keeping the wires separate. We begin a careful descent, making sure the wires stay connected to each charge. Jim signals Kurt and me underwater as to the locations of each explosive. Each charge has to be angled correctly, creating the maximum explosive power to remove sections of rock Jim has selected.

Carefully, each charge is set while keeping the wiring from getting tangled. It takes about thirty minutes to get everything just right. Jim inspects each charge one more time before we head back to the surface. Schools of fish dart around the coral heads as we go about our business. We project ourselves up from the mouth of the lagoon, inspecting the cable along the way. We complete the installation and prepare for the first detonation.

We remove our gear, taking care not to pull on the cable coming out of the lagoon. Jim takes his time making the proper sequence of connections to the control box. Each charge must be synchronized to explode in a certain order, splitting the rock as planned. He double-checks his connections carefully before charging up the box. All of us wait patiently for the first sound of an explosion.

Jim acknowledges his readiness, "Make sure everyone is well aware." He flips on the power switch as eight stations on his panel light up. He counts down, "Three, two, one!" He presses the main ignition button. We feel the rumble from below, as a large mass of bubbles burst to the surface. A few fish from the detonation float to the surface. The lights on Jim's control box change to red, showing that all eight charges ignited.

"Damn, that was a good one! Now we need to wait at least thirty minutes before heading down to survey the damage. Everything should be settled by then," Jim remarks with vigor in his statement.

"Jim, you just enjoy your work too much!" I exclaim as we watch the bubbles in the lagoon settle out.

"Somebody has to have some fun around here!"

Thirty minutes of ribbing conversations, and it's time to enter the water to check the results. Five of us, including Kurt, Jim, and me, grab fresh tanks and put on our gear. We enter the lagoon, noticing from the surface that the cavern entrance has been altered. Everyone signals that they are ready and down into the lagoon we travel. As we get closer to the entrance, I can see large sections of rock lying on the ground at the bottom of the cavern opening. The top of the cavern is opened up entirely from the blast. The explosives did a great job of breaking out the boulders. The opening is significantly enlarged from the blast. The hardest job is about to begin.

I notice Kurt heading into the cavern. As I watch, a section above him begins to fall. Debris commence to trickle from the fractured rock. Kurt's unaware of the danger as he continues to enter. He doesn't notice the instability of the section above him. I try desperately to get his attention before he enters into the cavern. Lunging towards him out of desperation, I accelerate as fast as I can. As I swim closer, the section above him let's go! It falls, pinning him on the rock below it. I look at Kurt as I approach him, noticing the grimacing pain on his face. Blood is beginning to flow from the thigh area of his leg. I bang on my tank, des- perately attempting to get the attention of the rest of the divers behind me. They notice my activity as I motion for help.

They rush over as we struggle to remove the section of rock off of Kurt. The rock will hardly move! I signal one of the divers to go to the surface and get two long steel wedge bars. The diver pushes off and heads quickly to the surface.

Kurt is doing fair, but his leg is noticeably bleeding at the thigh where he's pinned. I check his air gauge noticing he still has two-thousand pounds of air pressure in the tank. It's an adequate amount of air and should give us time to get him loose. I just pray his leg is not broken with internal vascular damage.

The diver returns quickly with two pry bars. I signal Jim to pull Kurt when we lift the with the pry bars. The three of us wedge the two bars as best we can, pushing with all our might. The rock gives slightly and Jim manages to pull Kurt from under the section of debris.

I see his leg has a deep laceration along with other multiple contusions. The laceration is above the knee about four inches in length. It appears as a flap of skin cut deeply by the rock. We get Kurt to the surface quickly attempting to hold pressure on the wound. Adrian and Liana look on frantically as we get Kurt to the water's edge.

He removes his mouthpiece and suggests with a touch of humor, "Not to worry; it's only a flesh wound."

"That's Kurt: always making with the jokes," Adrian says grimly.

We get him out of the water while checking to see how serious his wound is. The laceration is fairly deep, but no obvious major vascular damage. We check movement of his leg for the possibility of a fracture. Nothing appears to be broken, so we wrap the leg in clean towels and carry him back to camp. I can't resist the temptation to harass him on the way as I think to myself, "How lucky we are that Kurt didn't die today."

Malik has an emergency medical kit on board the ship and retrieves it. It contains most of the essential supplies we need to clean Kurt up.

Catalina remarks, "I worked as a nurse for a few years in Spain, so let me stitch his leg up before he bleeds to death."

"Besides my wife, you're the only other person here I would trust to do that."

She opens up the kit preparing the contents. "Let's just hope it won't get infected," Catalina answers as she begins to stitch the wound.

Malik gets the proper items out of the kit for Catalina. Kurt does his best to fight off the pain as he tenses with every movement. I get a bottle of rum from his crate. Catalina proceeds to pour a small amount over the incision.

"Hot damn that hurts!" Kurt yells out in a thunderous tone. "Leave some of that for me!"

"I can't let it get infected." Catalina reflects. "If you keep moving, I just might end up stitching the wrong parts!"

"Go ahead, I'm just letting off a little steam. It's just stupid bad luck!"

Kurt begins to drink as Catalina stitches up the wound. The more he guzzles the rum, the funnier things get.

He begins to sing Mexican love songs in a voice that is quite revolting, "My little Senoritas's, come home with me!"

We continue to support his drinking, hoping he'll pass out soon. It takes a while, but he soon falls asleep as Catalina finishes the stitches and wraps the wound in sterile dressings.

"We need to return to the lagoon to survey the entrance. It's time to launch the two-man sub to begin the cleanup," I beckon the people standing around.

Returning to the lagoon, we begin the tedious job of removing debris. Malik rigs a cable from the ship's crane. It's the only way we can drag larger rocks from the opening of the cavern. He rigs the cable so it will pull the larger sections of rock easily. The day expediently continues on, as progress is made on the opening. Several teams of divers are sent down throughout the day, removing sections of rock and coral. I estimate it should take ten to fifteen good days to complete this opening. Equipment eventually will be taken inside and setup in the cavern.

Looking at the sky to our south, Jim calls attention to it, "Have any of you noticed the eerie darkness and occasional lightning to our south?"

"It looks like we could be in for some nasty weather," I answer looking toward the sky. I holler to Malik, who's on a catwalk aboard the ship, "Malik, tune in the weather. See what's coming from the south."

He disappears for a few minutes, then excitedly returns to the catwalk, "The tropics are singing! We be in fa a bad storm Tony. It be up on us mon!"

"Pack it in. Malik, get the ship ready to move. If this system's bad enough, the ship could break up on the island. You're going to have to fight it out on the sea. Pull the anchors and get it moving!"

I quickly glance around, noticing the loose gear, tents, and equipment having to be fastened down. It will be a catastrophe to lose any of it. The tents have to be pulled apart. They could never hold up to high winds.

"Jim, get half the people here to help you take down the tents. The rest of you, help me get this gear strapped down."

Catalina questions my orders, "Where are we going to go? We have to get out of the storm!"

"There's twenty tanks. The cavern is the only refuge available to get out of its path. We may as well get used to being down there." Everyone barely moves with the idea of sitting in a dark cavern. "Times wasting! Let's get it done!"

I look over at the Sea Jewel as it begins to move towards the ocean. Everyone on board is scrambling to clamp everything down. The winds are picking up as the storm inches towards the island. The air begins to get cooler, and that familiar scent of rain arises. Lighting begins to flash. The lightning display is preceded by the rumble of thunder.

"We haven't got much time. The weather is approaching quickly. Just down the tents and chuck whatever rocks are in the area on top of them. Tie down the generators and the compressor. Someone get Kurt to the lagoon. We'll get him inside first," I bark out commands as I toss large rocks onto a downed tent.

"What about Steve and his helpers?" Catalina asks.

"I'm sure their looking for a shelter. Anyways, there's no time to look for them."

With the equipment strapped down, all of us begin to head to the lagoon. Lighting streaks against the sky as the rain begins to fall. The sky grows darker as the first ten divers, including Kurt, disappear underwater. Wind begins to gust bending trees with its force. Waves begin to break savagely in the lagoon. Eight of us remain, including Adrian and Liana.

Liana says in a somber voice, "I can't do this! I don't even know how to swim!"

"You have no choice sweetheart, there's no place else to go," Adrian pleads with her.

Liana looks in fear at the waves as they break against the rocks. She reluctantly allows Adrian to help her strap on a tank.

"I'll take her down with me. Liana, just breath normally through the regulator and don't panic. Press your hand against the mask and blow through your nose to equalize your ears when your ears begin to hurt. I'll help you the entire way. Just keep your eyes on me," I instruct Liana as Adrian buckles the final strap. We help her into the water as she begins to breath from the regulator. The waves force her to struggle as I enter the water and grip her by the arm. Her expression is teeming with fear. I get her to look into my face, "Where going under now. Just keep your eyes on me and don't panic. I'm not going to let go of you!"

She nods nervously with a feeling of utter apprehension. We drop about ten feet as she begins to push against me in an attempt to return to the surface. I make eye contact with hers. I pinch my mask against my nostrils to demonstrate how to equalize her ears. She follows my example and begins to calm down.

Looking into her eyes, I point to her ears and give her the 'OK" sign. She quickly returns the symbol as we continue to descend. I grasp her arm tightly, making sure she feels secure. Her eyes lock onto anything that wiggles as we slowly approach the bottom. Adrian and Catalina drop beside us from above giving Liana a bit of relief. Liana loosens her grip on my arm as her panic subsides. The remaining four divers gather near us.

A few divers, including Catalina, had the intelligence to grab underwater flashlights before leaving the surface. The entrance to the cavern beckons us as we kick our fins towards it. The eerie darkness deepens as I strain my eyes to look within. Catalina clicks on the flashlight giving the entrance some visibility as the storm above us darkens our surroundings. Our bubbles embrace the ceiling of the cave, cascading to seek the deepest crevice. We venture forth into the darkness with all flashlights illuminating the coral and rocks in front of us. The beams reflect off an occasional fish and particles of plankton. An occasional stingray flutters off the bottom as we progress inwards.

The cavern begins to widen as we enter the substance of the main cavern. We make a slow climb, ascending inside the cavern. Finally breaking the surface, we gather our bearings as to the direction of the ledge. Catalina aims her flashlight to the point where the rock ledge meets the water.

"There's our way out," Catalina reflects as she steadies the light.

"I'm ready to get out!" Liana informs anyone listening as she spits the regulator from her mouth.

"It's going to be a lot safer in here for the next several hours. Malik said it's a bad tropical depression that's moving directly over us. I would rather be down here than on the Sea Jewel with them," I try to reassure Liana as we swim towards the ledge.

"It's ok. I just want to get out of this water," Liana speaks with a nervousness to her voice. She coughs a bit from a slight bit of water that enters her throat.

Catalina and Liana are the first to struggle out of the water, leaving their tanks on the rock edge. I loosen the tank straps from Liana, giving her the freedom to climb out of the water herself.

"Come on Liana! Give me your hand and we'll pull you up," Adrian reassures her.

She extends her hand as they pull her from the water. The rest of us endeavor to get out of the water, pulling our equipment behind us. The cavern resonates the sound of our voices with a serene echo. Background noises of dripping water and splashing add to the mix. The inside of the cavern will take a bit of getting used to. Joining the others, we settle down to wait out the storm; picking a ledge to rest and reflect upon.

"Partners. It's not the Riviera, but it will have to do," I attempt to add relief to the situation.

"This is going to be home for a while, so we better get used to it now," Kurt reflects to all who will listen. "Liana honey, are you all right now?"

"Yes dad. I have to admit. I was petrified. All I could think about was sharks!"

"Uncle Tony wouldn't let anything happen to you. If my leg wasn't banged up, I would have been right beside you."

Hours drift by as we wait for the impact of the storm to pass. The echoing noises within the cavern take a bit of getting used to. An occasional scurrying animal can be heard in small crevices among the rocks. A far off sound begins to emerge that doesn't fit the sounds we have been hearing. It's distant at first, but gradually gets louder.

Kurt quiets everyone, "Quiet. There's something heading towards us from that branch of caves."

Silence is achieved quickly as we listen. Far off we hear the sounds of rocks tumble like someone or something is moving them. Our ears strain in the darkness almost picking up our own heartbeats. Again, we hear movement in the same direction; this time closer. I slowly grab a flashlight and prepare to flip it on in that direction. The mysterious sound in this darkness gives way to a vivid imagination. Could an animal be foraging in a cavern like this? How would it have gotten in here? My imagination begins to work overtime on me.

Suddenly, I hear a sound a bit more familiar. It sounds like a voice. A distant mumble, but a human voice all the same. Could a person be living in this cavern?

Kurt whispers, "Tony, turn on the light."

I aim it in the direction of the sounds. Pressing my thumb on the switch, the light snaps on. I maneuver the beam to catch sight of anything. A light in the distance starts to appear. I adjust the light to get any sight of what or who is approaching.

A voice in the distance echoes around the cavern, "Who's down there?"

I whisper to everyone, "Don't say a word."

The beam from their light makes contact with ours. I can barely make out two, maybe three forms moving down from the caves above.

"Will someone answer me?" The voice broadcasts again.

This time, there is a familiar tone to the voice. I answer, "Steve, is that you?"

"Ten four, good buddy!" he hollers from above.

"How in the hell did you get in here?!?"

"The storm drove us into a cave up in the top of this mountain. We decided to follow it back; just to see where it went."

"Partners! We got another way out! Damn glad to almost see you guys!"

Kurt adds with a sarcastic tone, "When my leg gets better, I might just have to do a little butt kicking after that stunt. You had the girls about scared to death! Thought there was a bear heading down here."

"Just us."

As night approaches, we return back to the lagoon's surface. The storm has toppled a few trees creating a challenge in camp. A generator is damaged from branches that fell on it. Time will tell if we can fix it. Some tents are found in mud puddles, making them uninhabitable for the night. We put together a few tents for temporary shelter. Malik returns, but he and his crew remain on board.

The work ahead of us is going to be dangerous and hard. If we work steadily, it should take ten days to get the bulk of the entrance clear. A lot of debris has to be moved in a short period of time.

Jim estimates it will take two more rounds of explosives to make the cavern entrance big enough. After each detonation, all the debris will have to be moved before the next explosive charge is set. Each round will get smaller in charge as Jim works his demolition magic.

The next day, it takes several hours to finish removing the debris from the first round of detonations. The small submarine helps out tremendously, removing smaller sections of rock. What the sub can't move, Malik manages to remove with the crane.

The debris from the first round of explosions is finally moved. It's time for a second round of explosives. Jim configures the plastic charges, needing only six detonations to do the job. Jim and I get our gear ready as Malik helps with the explosives. We enter the lagoon carefully, taking the charges to the bottom. The sections of rock that still need to be removed are further into the entrance. I aim a flashlight as Jim sets the charges into the rock. He carefully wires each one and checks them for the proper angles. One last check and it's back to the surface for both of us. We climb out of the lagoon preparing for the next blast. Jim connects the cable wires to his control box, as before, and connects the power. All the lights glow indicating a go for detonation.

Jim counts down, "Three, two, one!" and presses the main button. The ground rumbles and again the lagoon spews forth a large mass of bubbles. The second round of explosives has detonated flawlessly.

The four of us wait one hour before heading into the lagoon.

I instruct everyone, "Stay in back of Jim and I, until it's all clear. We don't want to have another accident like the one Kurt just endured."

Jim grabs his tank and mentions before jumping in, "Hopefully, this round of explosives will remove the largest remaining bulk of rock."

Climbing into the lagoon, we begin our descent toward the wreckage. We approach the area, noticing how extensively the explosives have annihilated the entrance. Except for a few jagged areas, the opening may just be wide enough for the sub. I signal Jim with a thumbs-up as we gaze into the entrance.

First we examine the top of the cavern, making sure loose sections don't exist. Jim notices a crack line along the left top side, but the rock appears solid. Jim writes on a board, 'Remove with the next set of explosives.' We give it the all clear, returning back to the surface.

Over the next few days, it takes us a tremendous amount of work to remove the rubble. Debris have to be taken further out from the entrance of the cavern, in order to keep the opening clear. The job is almost finished. One more round of explosives should give us the opening we need.

Liana announces in an arousing voice, "We have prepared a special meal. Hope all of you are hungry?"

Everyone conveys an agreeable message. A good meal is exactly what we need.

Jim remarks, "I'm glad to hear that someone has cooked. All of us are ready for a great dinner and a little relaxation."

Adrian and Liana brings out a few covered dishes, placing them in front of several people. They uncover the dishes revealing freshly caught grouper fillets that look delicious. Catalina enters with two more covered plates placing the first in front of Malik.

He pulls off the cover jumping back out of his chair yelling, "It be alive!"

On his plate sets a coiled snake in a strike position. Most likely one of the rubber ones he had earlier. Everyone in the room laughs hysterically. Finally, someone has gotten back at him.

Catalina stands smirking with arms folded, "You deserve that, Malik!"

"Bash it up mon; yah did dat wit Jamaican style!"

"Now, after you promise me that your pranks are on hold, you may eat."

"Me think mon, me just lost me appetite," Malik responds as he stares at the snake in front of him.

Catalina deserves a gold medal for that prank. Not too many people have got- ten Malik as good as she just did. The food finds its way into our stomachs, and is well appreciated. Fresh fish may be in abundance here, but it's still much more than we're used to.

Kurt clears his throat, "I can't stay cooped up any longer. I'm hell bent on getting back to work."

"If the leg is feeling better, I have just the job for you partner," I reply.

He works his way to a standing position, "Let's go. We're burning sunlight."

His wound is healing nicely, so we allow him to fill scuba tanks. If I don't give him some kind of job, he'll probably throw his gear on and re-injure his leg. The man is just too stubborn for words.

Steve and several others have been busy taking measurements around the island. He reminds me, "I'm going to take some equipment into the cave today. It appears as if we can fit some of the equipment through it."

"A lot of material needs to go. Take whoever you need, and see how much gear you can get down through the opening," I remark.

"I'll start working on it right now."

"John Mathews and Ray Watson are already in the cavern setting up the generators and wiring. They are going to need the generator soon, so hopefully you can get it to them. Power and lights will be the first convenience we need."

Steve tips his glasses forward on his nose as he thinks aloud, "An exhaust system will also have to be set up to remove any harmful fumes from the cavern. I should have the stealth system connected and running by the time we're ready to move underground."

Steve sets off with four people in an attempt to get the generator down into the cavern through the cave. It will save us a tremendous amount of time.

It's time for the third round of explosives. Jim rigs three detonators for the next set of explosives. The two of us dive into the lagoon and connect them with the same care as before. We return to the surface. Jim detonates the charges with the same enthusiasm as the first time. The explosives make only a slight vibration, spilling forth a foam of bubbles.

We return to the cavern entrance after waiting the proper amount of time. The explosive charge has taken out the rest of the jagged entrance. The rubble protrudes around the base of the cavern freshly removed from the cavern sides. The fish that normally dart around the entrance are absent. Looking into the cavern, I imagine in my mind the submarine entering into its depths. It may be a tight fit, but I estimate the opening is large enough.

We return to the surface satisfied with the results. The diving teams are put to work. Everyone needs to lend a hand. The debris is still in our way, and has to be removed. Malik sets up the crane, and the operation begins again. Rock and coral continues to be pulled from the entrance. The work continues as the entrance takes on a new appearance.

In the cavern, work is moving along steadily. Electricity has been established in the cavern with the generator being hooked up. The fumes are siphoned through a connection of tubes along the cave to the surface. The interior of the cave has lights for the first time in its existence.

Steve Roward finishes programing data into his system. It takes a few extra days to get all of his equipment set up in the cavern. He works diligently connecting the systems together, making sure each system interacts properly. We use an area of the cavern having the least amount of moisture for his equipment. Plastic sheets from the ship are hung in order to keep any further moisture from dripping on anything.

Steve makes his final connections, giving the system power for the first time. He spends the next several hours making final adjustments and entering the final programs. It's now time for the big test.

Along with his equipment, Steve constructs a computer program that taps into the government's satellite tracking system. It's illegal, but he insists it cannot be traced. He utilizes the program to test his stealth system.

The island appears normal without displaying the activity, camp, or ship in the lagoon. The system works! Steve has created the illusion of a peaceful, uninhabited island. A stealth island!

Steve informs us, "The system is now working, but it needs to be updated every so often to make sure it's accurate. Then it just has to be monitored."

What had seemed like a dream only a short time ago, is now reality. The island has now become home base for our network of operations. We still have to move the main camp down into the cavern, but the hardest work is behind us. Tonight we need to celebrate big time!

Carlos is contacted to get his team ready. It's time to shanghai the submarine. He will contact Captain Butler to get his group ready. In three days we will take the ship back to Jamaica. From there we'll fly to Cancun and begin preparations for the next phase of our operation.

OPERATION SUBMARINE

The crew spends part of the day catching lobster around the island. The area is abundant with marine life. Clams and shrimp are gathered, adding to the feast. We all plan to celebrate tonight in style.

Most of the camp has been moved into the cavern. An area outside the cave entrance remains as an observation post. All the tents are moved into the cavern, along with the provisions. Malik sets up a stereo system in the cavern that gives it a home-like atmosphere. John and Jose complete the lighting, giving the cavern a complete display of illumination. It's a good night to kick our feet up and celebrate what we have accomplished.

Kurt begins the night with a toast, "All of us have worked very hard these past few weeks to complete Starpoint. I have to say to all of you….It's worth it!"

You would think we were at Carnegie Hall by the sound of everyone cheering. The sounds bounce around the cavern echoing back into the smallest passageways.

I add to Kurt's toast, "This is the pivot point of our operation. If the world government won't stop this lottery, then by God, we'll stop it for them!"

Kurt waves his hands to quiet everyone down. "There is only one thing missing in this cavern." He hesitates, "It needs a submarine!"

At this point I feel like the cavern is going to shake apart from the noise. The cheering echoes even louder. If the cavern stands up to this, nothing will shake it apart.

Malik motions for my attention. "De food be Likky-likky. Let's eat, mon!"

Malik is right, the food at the table is a sight. All of us eat in grand style for the first time in a long while. My thoughts focus on the poor sections of the world having little food. With our efforts, may their stomachs be filled.

It's the first time in quite a while I feel like relaxing. Catalina starts the dancing off with an old song by the great Jimmy Buffet.

She strolls over to me and pulls me off my tail bone. We dance for a quite a long period of time, and the music begins to wear us out. The floor of the cavern is not the greatest dance floor, but we manage.

As the night draws to a close, I decide to make an announcement. "In two days, half of us will leave this island for Cancun. The rest of you will remain here to finish alterations on the cavern. Our next operation is not going to be an easy one. Any mistakes we make, will cost us our lives!" I hesitate to make sure I'm well heard. I continue, "Taking this submarine will place us on the government's hit list. If anyone wants to back out now, it's time to do so. Just tell us, and no questions will be asked. No one will think any less of you. I can't say this loud enough: Dangerous times lie ahead!"

Kurt adds with a laugh, "I'm the only one that has spilled any blood around here. All of you have had it easy."

That remark gets him hammered with a barrage of objects. "Ok! Ok, I give!"

I continue, "I also want to thank everyone for your help and support. All of you are the greatest. All except for Kurt."

"Amigo! That's cold," Kurt snickers with his usual boastfulness. He folds his arms in front of his chest raising his eyes towards the ceiling. "The gods will punish you for that one."

Mocking Kurt is becoming my favorite pastime. The big fellow takes everything in stride with his amusing sense of humor. A better friend could not be had.

The cavern's interior takes a bit of getting used to. The sounds within echo, giving an uncanny feeling of unnaturalness. An occasional fish jumping within the cavern or a bat flapping its wings takes away from the normal sounds. It takes a while to get used to sleeping within these walls. Now and then, I just have to go outside. The fresh air outside in the tropics does me a world of good.

Two days roll by as the cavern is organized with last minute changes. A satellite dish from the ship is mounted outside at a high elevation. Steve needs a better monitoring dish for his equipment. The stealth system performs flawlessly. Most of the important alterations in the cavern have been completed.

The time to leave the island is drawing near. Malik manages to get the ship ready for the voyage. Jim and half the crew plan to remain here keeping the island safe and secure. The rest of us will take the ship to Jamaica, then fly to Cancun to meet with Carlos, Kyle, and the rest of the team. Catalina, Liana, Adrian, and a few others will stay in Cancun. Sometime after the first lottery is over, we should be able to see them again. I will not risk their lives with the situation we are about to enter into.

We pull anchor around ten o'clock am, signaling goodbye to the group on the island. They set off a few flares as a signal of good fortune. It's a clear day, and we should make great time on the sea. The next time we see this island, our transportation should be under the ocean. At that time Starpoint will be a welcome sight.

The first night on the ship is a restless one. I can't shake the thought if something goes wrong with snatching the sub, we probably won't live to talk about it. Even if we are captured, they will execute us as punishment. This operation is still worth taking the risk—especially if we can save lives.

Kurt confronts me on deck. His limp is almost gone.

"You're walking damn good these days."

"Yeah, I don't think I ever thanked you for pulling me out of that cavern."

"Hey, what are pals for? Anyways, you pulled me out of a few hairy situations in the past."

I can tell something is bothering Kurt. His general mood is different. I decide to inquire, "What's on your mind?"

He hesitates, and then speaks slowly, "If anything happens to me, will you make sure Adrian and Liana are well taken care of?"

"Hey! First of all, nothing is going to happen to you and of course they'll be taken care of."

Kurt has never been uptight before. He's definitely in a strange state of mind. I have to ask the question, "It's not like you to be uptight. What's really the problem?"

"I know, but when I was pinned by that rock, all I could think about were my girls."

Kurt's showing a different side of himself. He has always been fearless. It must be married life bringing out his vulnerability.

"As long as I'm around—nothing is going to happen to you."

"Ditto, partner!"

The both of us stare out at the sea without saying another word. The ship glides along as the waves break against the hull. The whitecaps of the waves flow in a oscillating rhythm all their own. The front of the ship is being escorted by a few dolphin, swimming in their unique ritual pattern. Seagulls hover over the railings anticipating a quick bite of food.

The ship finally makes it to Jamaica. The waters are crystal clear as we pull into port. We anchor where Malik keeps it when moving freight. No time is wasted securing the ship, locking it tight, and grabbing our belongings. Our next stop will be Cancun, Mexico. Malik latches down the final items and joins us as we make our way to the airport. The Sea Jewel will have to stay docked until the need for her arises.

Twenty-four of us in groups of four or five people disburse in separate directions. I may be paranoid, but any attention to a large group may be costly. Traveling with the girls as couples definitely keeps any unnecessary awareness of our actions to a minimum.

It's not long before our plane lands in Cancun. Carlos meets us at the baggage claim area with one of his typical greetings, "Aloha, amigos! What a fine looking group of tourists. Kurt, looks like you developed a funny walk."

"Well, let's just say, I have to watch out for falling caves."

"I can tell you now, you won't live that one down for a while."

"Yeah, I could see that one coming. Just another stroke of bad luck for the old Kurt," He replies giving his best sneering facial expression.

"Well, let's get back to the bar, everyone's waiting."

A quick drive through Cancun brings us back to the Casa'de la Parrot, one of the few bars in town that has remained open through the last few turbulent years. Kyle and his team have already gathered and are anxious to discuss plans. We waste no time getting down to facts.

Twenty-two of us assemble in the backroom of the bar. It's time to organize and confirm our ensuing plans. The next phase of this operation is about to unfold. Hijacking this sub is going to take a great deal of planning and concentration. This sub will allow us to move quickly from continent to continent in our efforts to save condemned individuals. If a central continental land grid area is chosen by the lottery, we will add land vehicles to our operation. The submarine is a necessary first step.

Kyle stands up, pulls a few notes together, and begins. "While most of you were in the Caribbean, Carlos and I investigated this sub. It's the U.S.S. Constellation, a nuclear submarine built and used by the United States just after the last

Gulf War incident. In the year 2060, it was reconditioned to be a working, and fully functional relic of its era. It was built to be an attack submarine, but later was re-conditioned to belong to a Benjamin-Franklin class of subs. It was used by Special Forces and SEAL teams. The missile spaces have been converted to living accommodations and storage areas." He hesitates a moment to look at his notes. He begins again, "The length of this sub is three-hundred-and seventy-seven feet, the beam is thirty-four feet, and the displacement is about seven-thousand-eight-hundred tons. Originally, it could only travel at around twenty-five knots, but with the new upgrades it will exceed fifty knots. That's almost sixty miles per hour at top speed. It will hold almost three-hundred people with the new accommodations. At a bare minimum, it will take ten people to operate her."

Kurt interrupts, "How are we going to get people back from the beach to the sub?"

"I have already worked on a solution to that problem. We will attach four or five skip boats to the top area of the sub that can be released easily, one at any time. The motors and gas tanks will be sealed within the boats, so no damage will result from being underwater. These skip boats can be released above or below the water. They're fast, completely camouflaged, and can hold twenty-five people on each one. With those, we should be able to get people out of an area quickly. Carlos will explain the procedure."

Carlos clears his throat, stands up on his large frame, "Amigos, the Sea Jewel, will act as a holding area further out in the ocean. We use the skip boats to take people back to the sub. We fill the sub with rescued people, then travel to sea to unload them onto the ship. We repeat this operation many times, saving muchos people. The military people guarding them, we will dart with a drug. If people charge our skip boats, we dart them, too. If any problems occur, then we pull the plug. We will always work at night so we have a better chance."

I had to inject a question. "How many people do you think we can save?"

"With the equipment we have now…maybe fifteen-hundred. Two-thousand tops."

"Well, it's better than none at all!"

Kurt injects, "Let's talk about snatching this sub. How will we take it without getting caught?"

Kyle raises an eyebrow, strokes his beard, and begins, "On a weekend, it won't be too difficult. There should be only ten to twelve guards to knock out with our darts. I can have the sub underwater and moving in ten minutes. Steve just has to have his stealth system up and working within minutes. If not, we won't make it out of the harbor. We'll be visiting Davy Jones locker."

Steve nods to Kyle, answering, "It should only take me five minutes to make this big ton of metal disappear. I've worked the bugs out of the system."

"No! It has to be less than five minutes to guarantee a safe getaway."

Steve takes in a larger breath of air, "Then I'll make sure it's up in less than five."

"Good. We can't afford any mistakes. I guarantee it will cost us our lives."

The meeting goes on for another two hours, and details are hammered out. Carlos demonstrates the high-powered dart guns we will use to take out the guards.

"Senors, these guns can hit the eyeball of a cat at 100 meters. The drug takes effect mucho fast. They won't know what hit them for five to six hours. High powered, accurate, and then it's siesta time."

I interject into the discussion, "If anyone wants to find out how fast this drug works, just stand up and bend down. Get ready to kiss the floor. You'll have about two seconds to think about it."

Kurt adds his usual amusement to the conversation, "Malik needs a good nap. Demonstrate it for us compadre."

Malik wiggles down further in his chair, "No mon. I'll put a Jamaican curse on you!"

"We won't shoot you with it Malik. Just take my word, it will kick your butt, faster than you can imagine." My radicle exchange drives home the point.

Carlos continues, "We can also use them later when we begin the rescue mission. Gracias, amigos." He sits down satisfied with his input.

"Carlos and a few select people are leaving within an hour to drive the guns and equipment to an area just west of the submarine, which is on display in North Carolina. All of us will meet Carlos there early Saturday morning. Two days from now, we will hijack the U. S. S. Constellation and head to Starpoint island." I announce.

The remaining time is spent deliberating possible problems and scenarios in regard to the submarine. We finalize the discussions with a toast to a successful mission.

"Raise your glasses," I give everyone a few seconds to honor the toast. "To the upcoming success of our mission. May we all return to Starpoint victorious!" The drinks are consumed with a roar of camaraderie. Everything now depends on Steve's stealth system. A failure of this system will be suicide.

Catalina and I decide to visit her family and enjoy each other's company. These past few months have brought us together like no other prior relationship in my life. We are becoming inseparable. It's going to be very difficult to leave her tomorrow. I don't know how long it will be before we see each other again. I look into her eyes and see the same desperation. It's something neither one of us want to talk about today.

Catalina's father, Diago Delray, is a pleasure to meet. His has a dark flaring mustache, eyebrows, and sideburns. He retains a full head of dark hair, cut in a longer military fashion. His strong sense of stability bestows a great feeling of warmth in his presence. His handshake is very firm and confident. This man must have been a great loss to the Spanish people when he had to leave Spain. I can infer that he maintains a strong sense of moral values. It most likely is the reason he fights this government and rejects its values.

Catalina's mother, Maria Delray, is as beautiful as Catalina. Her strong family values and charm is reminiscent of her family's heritage. I now appreciate where Catalina inherits her beauty. Her hair reflects the same dark sparkle and sheen. The curvature of her figure is almost youthful as she flows across the room. Her Spanish complexion glows from within with her natural beauty. She has an air of romance about her that makes you feel appreciated.

Most of the conversation during the meal involves politics. I stifle the discussion when it involves our operation. It will only create turmoil for them if they have direct knowledge of our plans. I corroborate a promise to her parents that Catalina will remain in Cancun. She will be safe with them. I have a feeling Catalina has disclosed a bit of information about our operation, but we do not talk about it. I explain to them; a new job is taking me out of the country for a while. The time with them is short but impressive. I felt like I have known them for years.

Catalina slowly walks with me outside after thanking her parents for the gracious hospitality. It's an awkward moment. I can't find the words to say goodbye.

"I've been dreading this moment for weeks now," I say with a great deal of anguish.

"Hush." She puts her finger to my lips. A tear begins to run down her cheek. "I don't want you to say goodbye. We will see each other soon."

As I gaze into her eyes aware of the obvious torment. I hold her tight, so I won't forget what it's like to hold her. Our goodbyes have to be short, or we will not be able to leave each another.

"Please go now. Unless I let you go now, I may not be able to." She says as tears begin to flow.

"I love you with all my heart. You know I'll be back," I say as I slide away from her. I watch her in my rear-view mirror as I pull away from their home. Tears are running down her cheeks as she carefully wipes them away. Driving away is one the hardest moments of my life.

I arrive at the Casa' de la Parrot and enter through the back door. The main group of draftees are gathering in the backroom of the bar. Fortunately, everyone seems be enthusiastic about the mission. Around midnight, all of us will leave on a flight to North Carolina and meet with Carlos and his group. The plans have all been discussed. It's time to set them in motion.

The submarine is kept on display at an area on the Cape Fear River, just south of the Battleship U.S.S. Carolina. Old Town, North Carolina is just a mile north of its location and Sunny Point military Ocean Terminal is just to its south. We have arrangements to meet at a location off of Highway 133, several miles from the sub. Carlos has the guns, darts, and Steve's equipment ready to begin operations.

At five o'clock a.m. we will commence our operation to hijack the sub. If everything functions as planned, by five-thirty a.m. we will be aboard the sub and heading towards Starpoint. Our plan is to enter the sub at five o'clock a.m., knocking out the guards as we enter. Steve has to begin the immediate start-up of his stealth system, and have it up and running in less than five minutes. The sub will maneuver through the south end of the Cape Fear River, traveling between Caswell Beach and Bald Head Island. In minutes we plan to be heading out to sea in a submarine that will be invisible to modern tracking devices. The next stop, if we make it, is Starpoint Island.

CONSTELLATION

Our flight leaves at 10 p.m., and takes approximately 2½ hours to reach an air-park in Wilmington, North Carolina. Last minute equipment is checked thoroughly as we finalize our preparations. If anything is missing or unreliable, our whole operation will be compromised.

Kurt establishes the check list. "Amigos listen up. I want all of you to carry only a small duffle bag containing a camouflage jump suit, night vision binoculars, a signal S-type radio communicator, and navy moisture proof shoes. Everything else you need will be at the check point with Carlos. There we will change out of our regular clothes and into these jump suits. Everyone knows your assignments; we've been over the plans a dozen times. If everything falls into place, we should be able to take this sub without a problem."

Kurt looks around to make sure everyone is listening. He continues, "I want Steve and his equipment on board first, so he can get this stealth system up and running. Kyle's team will get to the control room and concentrate on the subs mechanical operations. Tony's and my crew will take out the guards and begin cutting loose the sub's tie-down ropes. Carlos and his posse will take out any remaining guards within the sub and eliminate any personnel aboard. We need to flood down, having us below surface within ten minutes of boarding. We will then make our run for the sea. Tony, have you got anything else to add?"

"Yes I do. Kyle has been a nuclear sub captain for many years. We are tremendously lucky to have him with us. Once aboard the Constellation, all activities are under his command. He has personally picked members of his main crew, so they control the operation of this sub. All of Captain Butler's orders will be followed!"

Kyle speaks up as I mention his duties. "This sub has been checked out and is ready for sea at any time. They keep it this way in case of extreme weather conditions that may prompt them to move her. Once aboard the U.S.S. Constellation, I will take command and get us to Starpoint as quickly as possible. My orders on this sub are not to be questioned! Tony will act as my Lieutenant Commander; due to the diligence he has demonstrated in formulating this plan. Once we begin this operation, we carry it out to the end. No one stops and no one retreats! If everyone is ready then let's head out!"

Twenty-four of us thunder out the door, grabbing all the gear as we exit. Two cargo trucks have been dispatched to carry us to the airport terminal. We pile into the trucks taking all the equipment in hand. Double rows of bench seats carry our behinds to the airport in a two-truck convoy. Silence is maintained during the ride. The drive seems like an eternity. We board the plane on time, making a non-stop flight to a smaller airfield outside of Wilmington, North Carolina. Carlos previously rented two large cargo step trucks and will to have them ready for us at the airpark outside the terminal.

Our flight arrives on time, and we make our way out of the main terminal. The trucks are in the parking spaces just as Carlos had been instructed. Keeping an eye on the time, we check out the vehicles, making sure they are secure. The area is scrutinized for any unusual activity before we load. After careful inspection, we clamber aboard and head for Highway 133, just a few miles west of the submarine's holding area. Carlos and his three companions are instructed to meet us at a predetermined location off this highway. If there have been leaks of information about our operation, we will soon know it. Our trucks will either be stopped on the way or surrounded at this location. As careful as we have been, there's always a possibility of information leaking into the wrong hands.

Everyone remains fairly quiet as we travel. The anticipation of a problem weighs heavily on everyone's mind. The feeling in the air reminds me of some of our old navy operations. Everyone is nervous, but at the same time ready for immediate action.

We make our approach to the rendezvous area. At this time of night, the roads are empty. A left turn off of Highway 133 takes us to a small road heading directly towards the submarine. We drive approximately one mile, which leads to a small field. It resembles the area Carlos described, with instructions to meet.

As we approach the field, our headlights catch the reflection of a vehicle parked beside a tree. Only one vehicle can be seen as we enter. We stop about fifty yards and flash our lights three times, anticipating the proper reply. The driver flashes back twice, hesitates, and then flashes twice more. This is the signal we are waiting to receive. As we pull up, Carlos gets out of the vehicle and signals a big thumbs-up. We park the vehicle delivering everyone in preparation for the final stage.

Carlos remarks after a security check is achieved, "I hope it's only my amigos! I have a few darts loaded just in case."

I pat Carlos on the back with relief that he's here, "Partner, let's save those darts for the guards. I wouldn't want to leave anyone here to sleep it off."

"Well senor, all the guns are loaded and ready to pop a few hides. These darts should lay them out for a five hour siesta."

Kurt jumps out of his side of the truck, grumbling, "Let's get everything unloaded, and I don't want anything left behind. These trucks are rented under a fictitious name, so no trace can be made to any of us. I just don't want anything left behind that can even remotely be linked to us. Wipe everything clean and leave no fingerprints."

Carlos presents the weapons while taking a stance behind a truck. He instructs, "Check your weapons. Get into the jump suits." He inspects the weapons one at a time before handing them out.

Steve performs a final check of his equipment, making sure it is operating perfectly. This is the last time he has an opportunity to test this equipment before we are on board the sub. He diligently checks the connections with a glow light.

Kyle makes a quick sweep of the area, checking for any loose ends or forgotten items. He reassures us, "We shouldn't have any problems taking this sub. If Steve's equipment works without fail, we will be home free. Just stick to the plan and we should be good to go. It's time to double check everything and put ourselves to the test."

Malik looks around with a smile and comments, "I'm ready to get back to the islands, mon."

Kyle places his dark hood over his head and nods in agreement.

Breaking into three main groups, we have less than thirty minutes to get the sub ready for a crash dive. We walk three-quarters of a mile through a wooded area, utilizing night vision goggles to see our way. Ahead of us, just beyond the tree line, is a guard shack with four guards on duty. I gesture to Kurt, Malik, and Carlos, "Approach from three directions, and surround the shack." Each of us takes aim on a separate guard. I give the signal to fire. A slight hiss is heard as the guns engage. The four guards arch as the darts strike, causing them to collapse within seconds. One of them crawls for a second, then falls silent. I approach, motioning the others to hold their positions. Carefully I flip each body to check for consciousness. Each guard is out cold as the sleep agent accomplishes the intended affect. I execute a signal, engaging everyone to move forward. Carlos and Kurt cut all communication lines and signal equipment. Carefully we hold our positions as the lines are thoroughly clipped.

About two-hundred yards beyond us is the U.S.S. Constellation, looking as majestic as ever. Three other guards are on duty standing along the main dock. The glare of lights reflect off the hull of the sub as it remains stable alongside the dock.

Kurt quietly whispers, "There are others aboard the sub waiting to exchange watch duty. The time has come to get this job done."

"Let's move in." Kyle answers as we move silently towards the sub.

Creeping through the brush alongside the main walkway, we make our way closer to the guards. Carlos and his team kneel in position toward the front of the main docking area and prepare to get on the sub quickly. Kurt and I, with our troops, silently secure positions at the stern. Kyle, with his posse, waits patiently for the signal to board. It's time to take the Constellation.

I signal the teams. Three darts spring from their weapons, hitting the guards and dropping them where they stand. Carlos and his team leap into action, making their way quickly to the main hatch of the sub. Carlos takes a position in front of the hatch. Suddenly without warning, a guard leaps out from the starboard side of the sub.

"Get out of there Tim!" I bellow. A shot rings out that stuns all of us! The bullet clobbers a member of Carlos's team dropping him to the deck. The guard begins to take aim on another victim. Carlos swings around launching a dart that strikes the guard in the thigh. He drops his gun, stumbles, and falls silently to the deck. His weapon sprawls out in front of him. Tim pleads as the pain engulfs him, "I'm hit! I'm hit!"

It's now a race against time! The gun shot can be heard for miles, signaling the sub is under attack. Tim holds his abdomen, intensely bleeding on the deck. He moans from the pain, holding onto his abdomen.

"Someone help Tim out! The sub needs to be cleared quickly!" I shout out the orders.

The rest of Carlos's posse enters the sub's hatch. The rest of us, although stunned, hold positions on the sub's outer shell, waiting for the sub to be cleared. Malik rushes to Tim as he slouches over him in order to triage his condition. The wound is gurgling blood as Tim pleads, "Don't let me die." He turns his hand noticing the blood draining from his body.

Malik carefully pulls him towards the main hatch. His wound is traumatic, and he groans in pain while being slid along the deck. "Hold on mon. We take care of you," Malik reassures him.

Kyle and his team rush into position to enter the sub. He discloses with an air of concern, "I can begin start up procedures when we get the all clear. We need to get aboard!"

The clock is ticking as Steve gathers his stealth equipment near the opening. "I have to get to the bridge quickly and begin the start-up of this system." He wears a worried look on his face as he nervously pulls his equipment closer.

Suddenly, a muffled shot is heard echoing within the sub. Nervously, we stand disillusioned staring at the hatch. Thirty seconds click by and still no signal from the hatch. I approach the opening ready to enter myself when Carlos appears, "Amigos, It's all clear. Come aboard now."

With a wave of his hand he signals the all clear, allowing Kyle and his team to enter. They climb down through the hatch nearly ripping the side bars as they go.

Steve gathers his equipment and lowers it down through the hatch opening. He nervously enters the sub, taking care not to fall as he climbs down the steps. The stealth equipment is hurried into the bridge. Steve quickly begins the attachments.

On the deck, I instruct Malik, who is getting impatient while he helps Tim, "Get the injured team member below and give him some medical attention. Have someone help you lower him. The rest of you remain at your positions until the sub is ready to dive!"

I enter the sub, helping Malik with the injured team member. Tim grimaces in pain as we lower him through the hatch. His injury is very serious, and blood trickles down his right thigh. We locate the first bunk area and carefully lay him down in one of the bunks. He drifts in and out of consciousness as his face becomes pale.

I advise Malik as he applies pressure to the wound, "Do the best you can for him. I have to find Carlos and get this sub moving!"

"Jah mon. He's not looking good," Malik answers with frustration.

Carlos is one level below us, and he returns from the engine compartment. I sense his frustration and inquire, "Did anyone else get shot?"

"No amigo. We entered the dining room surprising a guard. He unloaded a stray shot when we darted him. Lucky for us, the shot did no damage. We darted three other guards. No one else is on board."

"Good. Have three of your team members carry them to the dock area outside the sub. Just don't kill any."

Carlos spins around on his sizable frame ducking lower than most of us to get through the door hatch.

I make my way to the control room where Steve is finishing the final connections. His monitors flash as he connects the last few cords together. "Systems coming up!" he pants working furiously to ensure availability.

"Let us know the second your system is up and running," I demand in an impatient tone.

"I should have it up in less than two minutes…just have to connect it to the subs antenna system."

"Good…it's in your hands now!" He wipes his forehead as he nervously makes the last few connections.

Kyle and his team already have the sub fully powered up. Last minute checks prepare the instruments for final dive readiness. Kyle appears cool as a cucumber as he glances at the pressure gauges. He glances over at me and asks, "Does Steve have his system up yet? I'm almost ready to pull the plug on the sub."

"He says less than two minutes, and we should be in stealth mode."

"I hope so. We can't get through the Cape Fear River without it. We'll be sitting ducks." He flips his glasses lower on his nose. "Get everyone on board now!"

"Those are the words I have been waiting for!"

I battle my way quickly to the hatch and climb out onto the deck. Everyone retains a foothold guarding the sub's position. For the moment everything remains quiet.

"Cut the ropes. Everyone get below!" My voice carries through the night air.

The lights along the Cape Fear River glimmer with the gleam of the slender crescent moon. Looking back towards the guard house, I peer through the darkness expecting to see activity. Nothing stirs.

Kurt signals back, motioning for everyone to get below. He discharges an order, "Get your buts into the sub! Last man down—seal the hatch."

Three men on my team have already detached the sub from the dock by cutting away the guide ropes. Everyone crams down through the hatch, taking refuge inside the Constellation. Kurt takes one more look around as he grips the sweaty hatch plate. In a final effort, he slams the hatch closed, spinning the wheel to engage the locks.

Kurt bellows from the top of the ladder as he double checks the hatch, "It's time to put on the Kick-Ass! Let's get this baby moving!" He acrobatically slides backwards down the ladder, landing with a thump as he hits the floor plates.

"It's now or never. I hope Steve has us on stealth," I reflect, feeling confident we may just make a getaway. I wipe away a bead of sweat that begins to irritate my eyes. The lights slightly flicker as power is redirected in the control room. We quickly make our way through the corridors until the control room is located. Making our way into the room, I locate Steve who is monitoring his system.

I invoke upon him hoping for the best response, "Are we on stealth mode?"

"Partially, but my signal strength is weak. I've got to connect it to a better source for signal reliability."

"Get it fixed now! We can't afford not to have it at one-hundred percent."

"The antenna is unreliable. I need to change it to the main frame of the inner sub."

"Do-It! We need to have it at max strength!" I contend, hoping for a better response.

Steve expediently begins to change the connections around. His nervousness escalates by the second. I begin to fear the worse as the sub will be an easy target with only one escape route to the ocean, the Cape Fear River.

Kyle orders as he strokes his beard, "Flood down to periscope depth. "Keep an even trim." Kyle's duty officer repeats the orders, "Flood down to periscope depth. Trim is set. All systems operational."

The sub rumbles as it releases air and submerges from its resting spot. We can feel the water break over the deck as the sub floods down to below the surface. A slight heaving motion begins to develop as the sub begins to move.

Kyle takes hold of a cross member and orders, "All ahead five knots, five degrees down bubble." The duty officer repeats the order.

The sub lurches slightly forward as the orders are carried out. We are heading to the mouth of the Cape Fear River without the protection of the stealth system. Steve continues to adapt his connections in hopes of a remedy. Kyle maintains his composure, but the tension in the air is as thick as molasses. By now an alert must have been sounded. The gun shot that occurred earlier on deck had to alert someone.

The bulkheads rock the sub slightly as they adjust to the new depth. The background hum of motors along with the occasional creak of flexing steel can be heard.

Kyle intensely questions Steve. "How are we doing on stealth?"

Steve answers nervously, "Give me thirty seconds to initiate it, and we should have this sub disappear off of all targeting devices."

"Let me know the second we're on stealth."

The radar officer interrupts, "Sir, we have a ship approaching from the Wrightsville Beach area actively pinging."

Kyle retains his composure, "How far are we from the Bald Head Island Inlet?"

"Sir…about one minute on our present course."

"Increase speed to twenty knots, stay on course."

The sub picks up momentum as we pass through the inlet by the Cape Island Lighthouse. We are entering the Atlantic Ocean as we pass Bald Head Island to our port side. Kyle grips the hinged handles of the periscope leaning in to get a good look.

Again the radar officer breaks the silence, "Sir, they are actively pinging us and closing!"

Suddenly, Steve hollers out, "We're up! The stealth system is working!"

Kyle leans back from the 'scope, pears over his glasses and remarks, "Just keep it up and running. I'm going to try and make our escape. Increase speed to twenty-five knots."

The duty officer again repeats the order. The sub rocks slightly as it picks up speed.

The radar officer illuminates as he looks up from his screen, "They are searching again. They've lost us, sir."

Kyle glances over at me and winks with an air of satisfaction, "We're on our way with only one casualty, and Steve's stealth system has created our escape route. Sometimes it just comes down to the wire."

With the immediate danger behind us, I file out of the control room to check on the injured team member. Weaving through the barracks hatch, I make my way over to his bunk. As I walk up, the men taking care of him have a look of despair on their faces. Malik is standing by his right side, doing the best to make him comfortable. Blood stained dressings are wrapped around his abdomen.

I ask, "How bad is he?"

Malik looks up and just shakes his head back and forth but never utters a word. A death of a fellow soldier is hard to take. The wounded man is Tim McGraw from Missouri. He was brought into our group by Carlos, who had known him for years. His wound is extensive with the bullet entering the right side of his abdomen just above his navel. The blood loss is obvious, causing him to slip into unconsciousness.

I sadly remark to Malik, "Do the best you can for him. Keep him comfortable and out of pain."

Malik nods in agreement as Tim quickly losses his battle for life. Malik's solemn mood is atypical for him, but understandable. The emotion in the room is very earnest, as a life hangs on the wire.

I make my way back to the control room to ensure we have escaped an absolute death. Steve is busy monitoring his equipment and fine-tuning its accuracy. Kyle has the sub running as smoothly as a fine tuned clock.

Kyle looks over at me and reflects, "We've passed out of the Cape Fear Inlet. The ship that was pursuing us, lost us as a target several minutes ago. In a few minutes, I'm going to drop us down deeper and begin a zig-zag pattern until we're out into the Atlantic. How's our wounded?"

"He's not going to make it. There is just too much blood loss and no way to stop it."

Kyle leans back taking in a deep breath and shakes his head. "He will always be remembered. It took guts to pull this job off. We did the best we could."

"I'll locate his family when the time is right and let them know how heroic he was."

He addresses his duty officer, "Ten degrees down bubble. Full ahead! Bow planes down!"

Turner responds, "Aye Sir."

"Sonar, have you picked up any more movement?"

"No sir. Just the activity to our aft."

"Good. We'll have a good run to the sea. Looks like we made it by the skin of our teeth."

Kurt approaches from a galley hatch and glances around the control room. He enthusiastically remarks with an air of confidence, "Looks like we made it. I knew you son of a bitches could pull this off."

Kyle turns himself towards Kurt answering, "We're not safe until I have this hunk of steel way out into the Atlantic! Then you can wipe the sweat off your brow."

A feeling of relief is settling over us as we make our way out into the Atlantic Ocean. The daunting spirit of all these men reinstates my expectations for the future. We have traveled a rough road to get to this point.

Suddenly, the radar officer announces, "Sir, I have a sonar signal approaching from the south."

Kyle raises his eyebrows, "How fast is she moving?"

"Twenty knots sir. She's actively pinging."

"Well, they discovered the Constellation is missing. Steve, this will be a real good test of your stealth hardware."

Steve looks over at me with a worried look on his face. "We should appear just like the ocean around us. A zig-zag pattern again may eliminate our wake."

Kyle takes in a deep breath and contemplates Steve's statement. "Begin zig-zag pattern. Head fifteen degrees north first. Make slow but distinct turns until further notice." Turner repeats Kyle's commands.

The sub rocks in response to the direction change. The mood in the room intensifies. Kyle walks over to a stretched out chart and begins to study it. He adjusts his glasses to focus in on the depths. "Sonar, what is your reading?"

"It's just actively searching, sir. They can't find our signature."

"Steve, you're a good man. Remind me to shake your hand when we are totally in the clear."

Steve hovers over his equipment as he fine tunes the display monitor. The readings appear normal and seem to be working as programmed. He composes himself as if a thousand tons has been lifted off his shoulders. He answers with a new air of confidence. "They can ping us all day and night without finding a thing. We are the proverbial 'needle in a haystack'."

"Just keep us on track. We don't need any more surprises. Sonar, keep me posted if anything changes."

The sonar officer replies, "Yes, sir. They're only randomly searching."

Ten minutes clicks off the clock as the sonar scope records no new activity. The sub continues to zig-zag on its coarse as we retreat from the mouth of the Cape Fear River. Sonar only records activity to our aft.

Kyle engages another order, "Ten degrees down bubble. All ahead thirty knots. Discontinue zig-zag coarse."

Turner repeats the orders. The sub shifts forward as we dive a bit deeper into the Atlantic. The momentum of the sub changes as the sub increases speed. The Atlantic Ocean is a large place to search for a sub that is camouflaged by stealth technology. I would give anything to read the newspapers tomorrow morning. Our escape is practically in the bag.

Malik appears from the hatch with a very somber look about him. He glances around the room and announces, "Tim be wit de lawd now; de bleeding not stop."

Everyone falls silent; you can almost hear a pin hit the floor.

Kurt suggests, "He will be missed. We just have to be thankful that the rest of us are alive." Malik nods his head in acceptance, and then walks back through the hatch.

Kyle remarks, "He seems to be taking it badly. Were they friends?"

"No, Malik just respects life so much, he has a bad time dealing with death. Even in the Navy he underwent a mood change whenever anyone died. He'll be alright tomorrow."

Kyle understands the explanation. I can read it on his face. Even Kyle, who faced tragedies throughout his career, hates to lose anyone in combat. It's the irony of battle.

"Tomorrow, when we get far enough out to sea, we can give Tim a proper burial. We'll have to use a torpedo tube."

I nod my head without saying a word. It isn't the best way to hold a funeral but under the circumstances, the only way.

The U.S.S. Constellation continues its trek out to sea without a hint of a problem. She is very well constructed for her day. It's too bad warfare was her main purpose. We just may just change her history.

Kyle keeps the sub at a steady pace, slowly increasing speed and depth as we head out towards the Caribbean islands. The Navy sure lost a great commander when Kyle made the decision to quit. He has nerves of steel, and doesn't flinch when a problem manifests itself.

I need to check out the inner compartments of the sub. Since it was converted for the Special Forces, all missile compartments have been changed over to storage and recreational spaces. The sub could easily carry three-hundred people with room to spare. Every effort has been made to make the most out of all this space.

I find Kurt in the galley cooking up whatever he can find. He gratifyingly stirs his creation as if he were in his own kitchen preparing a feast for the family. He tips his head forward to look up at me. "I've got a good brew of coffee going. Ham and eggs to follow. Pull yourself up a seat"

I have to laugh. His demeanor is cool as a cucumber. "You are certainly a piece of work. I could use a good meal right now."

"Give me a few minutes, ham and eggs it is. Hope you like powdered eggs?"

"Coffee is what I need right now. Looks like our plans have worked out so far."

Kurt gives me that sly facial expression that he's known for and answers, "Did you really think we were going to fail?"

I search my thoughts for a second, "When that shot rang out, I wondered for a second if the cavalry had arrived. The son of a bitch took me for a surprise!"

Kurt slightly smiles as he continues tossing sizzling ham in the pan. The coffee goes down great, but I can't say too much for the ham and eggs.

"I need some shuteye. Wake me in six hours." I grab a cot in the main barracks and fall asleep in an instant.

CHAPTER 8

1ST LOTTO

Radio reports we begin to receive, regarding the hijacking of the submarine U.S.S. Constellation, are insanely ridiculous. The media faults everyone from anti-government terrorists to government insiders. The insiders they imply are utilizing the sub for secret maneuvers. The media ravages this story with their normal idiotic hear say. The big puzzle on everyone's mind is how this large submarine just disappeared without a trace. As the reports continue to escalate, we find a bit of humor in their narration.

Accounts of increasesd rioting with savage anti-lottery demonstrations continue to esculate as the inaugural date draws near. Barbaric incidences of civil unrest flood the radio waves. From fire bombings in the Middle East to suicides in Europe, the public discloses their resentment to the lottery.

Kurt wakes me up right on time, holding a cup of coffee above my head. "Don't look now buddy, but you're on a sub heading towards the Caribbean."

"Partner, did you get any shuteye?"

"Yeah, but you know me; I can't get any real sleep with all this excitement going on."

I grab the cup of coffee out of Kurt's hand as I slowly raise myself up in the cot. After gaining some focus, I ask the first question that pops in my mind, "How's the sub running?"

"Great! Kyle has us somewhere along the northern Florida coast. His team is taking turns catching some Z's. About one more day and we should be in paradise."

I straighten up, stretching my back to get out the kinks. "I'm going to check things out. Need to wake up anyway." I head straight to the control room, bowing down to get through each hatch. I notice Kyle sitting near some spread out nautical charts. "Have I missed anything worth reporting?"

Kyle straightens his glasses as he looks up from a depth gauge. He reflects, "We have about six hours left until we reach Starpoint. There can be no radio contact made between the sub and Starpoint. I don't want to chance the possibility of our communications being monitored." He hesitates to glance at the charts. "Search vessels and planes will be up and down the eastern seaboard looking for any signs of the missing sub. If we break silence, they can still target us."

Steve speaks up, feeling more confident about his advice, "Kyle is right! It would be the only way our location could be compromised. The radio needs to stay silent."

"Glad to see everything is kosher. The sooner we can get there, the better." I acknowledge, giving respect to the captain. "Anyone see Malik?"

"He was in the pantry about five or ten minutes ago," Steve answers as he follows the patterns on his monitor.

"Thanks, partner. I need to speak with him about a special mission."

Finding Malik in the very place Steve spied him, I clap my hand on his shoulder. "Just the man I need to speak with."

"Ooo goes dere?" Malik spins around in a startled look on his face. "Tony, Lissen me nuh, you scare me!"

Malik is beginning to resemble his old self again after the funeral service for Tim McGraw. I take him aside to go over the details for of the next phase of our operation.

"The sub we have commandeered has to be outfitted on the outer deck with five or six skip boats. In the next few days, we have to get you and a few others to a location where you can catch a plane to Jamaica. We need you to get these boats!" I give him a second to absorb the information. "From there, you use the Sea Jewel to bring the skip boats and other supplies back to Starpoint. If any military ships notice the Sea Jewel, don't risk an approach to this island. Wait until the time is right."

"Me get yah anyting yah ask; jus don't leave if de government mon announces his first lottery," he exclaims in a worried tone.

I have to snicker a bit. "Malik, I couldn't leave without you! You're sailing our getaway ship."

"Jah, mon! The Sea Jewel will set them free."

"Malik, you're one of a kind. You never question a problem or deny a request. I think we'll keep you around here for a while. Go and get your people ready and pack for the voyage."

"You know me be ready, mon."

"I hope you can get everything and make it back in six to seven days. You can't fail at this, Partner. This whole operation depends on those boats." The seriousness in my voice drves home my point. I know he'll get this done.

Every now and then my thoughts drift, and I begin to think about Catalina. I have to be honest with myself and admit, I miss her badly. I can picture her great smile and beautiful eyes as I sat daydreaming about her. I can still picture her with tears in her eyes as I pulled away from her parents' home, unsure of when we would see each other again.

Time goes by rather quickly and before I knew it Kyle has us near Starpoint. His careful maneuvering has taken us through the channels near the island.

Kyle leans over toward the periscope, and with a slight smile on his face orders, "Periscope depth. Change speed to fifteen knots. Raise the scope." Turner responds and repeats the orders.

The periscope is raised as Kyle leans carefully against the eyepiece. He slowly makes a visual turn until he stops and gazes in one direction.

"There's your island. It looks just as peaceful and quiet as you described it."

Kurt questions him, "Are you going to take her directly into the cavern?"

Kyle leans back from the eyepiece. "It's going to take some fancy maneuvering, but it's time to take her in. Everyone to their stations. We don't need to scratch her up. Down periscope."

The relief on everyone's mind is obvious. We may have just gotten away with the hijacking of the U.S.S. Constellation. The stealth system Steve perfected works perfectly, giving us the invisible blanket to get here.

Kyle hammers out the next order as he pushes back from the scope. "All ahead ten knots. Let's keep to the channel."

The sub glides towards the cavern entrance. Kyle hesitates before making slight maneuvers.

The sonar officer reports, "Sir, ten knots and closing. Five-hundred yards to the entrance."

"Reduce speed to five knots. Five degrees down bubble."

The sub decelerates as the entrance is reached. The sonar officer reports, "Sir, we are entering the cavern."

Kyle shifts his weight to one side, "Get ready to blow ballast. Reduce speed to three knots."

A slight scraping noise is heard coming from outer shell of the sub.

Kyle leans over towards me disclosing, "It looks like the opening is just a little bit tight."

I nod in agreement as I wait for the next sound. About thirty more seconds clicks off the clock. "Full stop! Blow ballast!"

The sub rumbles as it breaks to the surface of the cavern. A faint sound of water sloshing across the deck is reassuring. For the first time in the cavern, the display of the sub surfacing must be magnificent.

As we climb out onto the deck of the sub, we begin to hear clapping from the ledge above. Jim and the rest of the individuals that stayed behind, begin to cheer and clap as we slowly disembark. I have to admit the feeling is quite exhilarating. It's great to be back at Starpoint without suffering any more tragedies.

Jim yells down from the cavern with an echo, "Great parking job! I need to get me one of those."

Kurt looks up from his best vantage point answering, "Yeah, but you couldn't afford the premiums on this baby."

"It's great to have all of you back here. Any trouble?"

"There were a couple of close calls. Tim McGraw was shot and unfortunately died later."

"I'm sorry to hear that. Come on up and tell us about it."

We disembark one at a time on a crudely made gang plank. I glance back at the U.S.S. Constellation as we step off the plank and admire how impressive it appears. It's an awe inspiring sight to see her in this cavern after all the planning we have accomplished. It's hard to imagine that we have achieved so much.

Walking towards the side wall, it strikes me how much extra work has been done inside the cavern. Lighting has been increased with flood lamps casting a brighter illumination within. Exhaust fans are operating removing fumes to the outside through the newly discovered cave. Even a crudely constructed bathroom is constructed utilizing tarps for privacy.

During dinner, we describe to Jim and the others how the operation unfolded. The plan hadn't gone as smoothly as we anticipated, but we pulled it off. Everyone feels a great deal of sorrow for Tim Mcgraw's death. He'll be sadly missed. It's a subject we do not dwell on.

We listen to news reports only speculating as to the whereabouts of the sub. The media continues their circus as the government dispels rumors regarding direct involvement with the missing sub. At the present time, no evidence has been found to link anyone or any group to the theft of the U.S.S. Constellation.

The rest of the night is spent evaluating the sub and planning the next phase. Our next operation entails preparing the submarine for the first rescue mission. Skip boats have to be placed on deck for quick release and quick attachment. They must be able to release above or below the water. If the lottery committee picks a land-based area, then our plans will have to be altered to accommodate the land surface.

I snap awake early to get Malik and his crew to the next set of islands. We take two of the smaller boats. The day is a bit overcast as we travel along the outer island. A few dolphins give us an escort across the open water. They playfully race along the front of the boat as if they are discovering a new game. It takes three hours to reach a small port with access to Nassau.

"Get everything we need and return as quickly as you can," I remind Malik as he slips out of the dingy onto a dock.

"You can count on me, mon. Everything be alright."

"God Speed."

Malik and his crew locate a boat heading to Nassau. From there, they will catch a flight to Jamaica. I return with Jim to Starpoint and begin the tedious job of welding supports on the deck of the sub for the skip boats. A few others begin to rearrange the interior of the sub's compartments to receive the large amount of people we plan to rescue.

The days creep by waiting for Malik and his crew to return. Everything on the sub has been completed. We just need the skip boats to finish making the final attachments. Steve's stealth system works flawlessly as we work diligently underneath the island's surface. Steve fine-tunes the system every so often, making sure it is working at peak performance. A flaw in its function could cost us everything.

Finally, on the sixth day, Malik's ship appears rounding the island's peninsula by our lookout. Malik and his crew inch the ship up into the lagoon, anchoring it as we did during earlier operations. Malik stands on the deck of the ship and flips back some covers, revealing five skip boats.

I holler up to him, "You've done it again! I knew we could count on you."

"Jah, mon. The skip boats are the best me find, but they run real good."

"Any trouble getting them?"

"No, mon. But me have to tell them, they be selling to a big company."

"Partner, I like the way you think."

With my remark, Malik breaks into a big smile and begins unstrapping the boats. He and his crew lowers them one at a time by use of the crane. The boats are maneuvered into the cavern by a few of us using scuba gear. The small sub works perfectly to guide the boats within the cavern. We begin attaching the skip boats to the sub's deck, making the final preparations for their use. The boats are kept sealed throughout the procedure so that the motors will start perfectly when needed. We work diligently to connect them, making alterations on the welding supports. They have to stay in place on the sub during transport, but release easily.

Suddenly, Steve frantically runs up to the gang plank yelling, "You've got to hear the news report coming over the radio…they're naming the first grid section!!" He runs back to the radio in the computer area and switches the speakers over from music to the radio.

The news report blasts across the speakers: "Today, the United Nations World Government has announced the selection for its first lottery. This area has already been sealed off by the U.N. military force, keeping its citizens in confinement. The area has been computer selected randomly by the officials of the United Nations Committee. The area selected is the Yucatan Peninsula in Mexico. Cities affected within the peninsula include Progreso, Cludad Del Carmen, Chetumal, Cozumel, Cancun, and areas as far south as Comalculco.

All of us freeze in our tracks as terror runs through our minds. The sudden fear that grips us cannot be imagined. All of us gaze blankly at each other in disbelief. They have just named Cancun as a target area!!

Kurt screams out with a ghostly cast to his face, "The son of a bitches are going to murder our families!"

My heart begins to beat frantically as a feeling comes over me that will haunt me the rest of my life. Catalina and her family are going to be executed along with most everyone's families. We stand paralyzed, staring at each other, completely in shock. The only woman in the world I truly love and adore is now marked to be executed.

Kyle responds to our terror, "We're going to launch now. Let's get your loved ones out of Cancun." He jumps up knocking over a crate. "No one's dead yet."

These words snap me to my senses. The intense feeling of terror and anger shakes me to the bone. I yell up to Steve, "Turn off that damn radio. We've heard enough!"

Kurt finds some inner strength, "Kyle's right! We are the only hope they have, so let's get this sub on its way to Cancun. Nobody is going to die while I'm still breathing!"

We frantically finish the attachments and connections for the skip boats. Carlos and a few others gather all the scuba gear, filling the tanks, and lower everything into the U.S.S. Constellation. All the final details including the skip boat supports are completed quickly as the sub is prepared to dive.

I plead with Malik, "Get your people together on the Sea Jewel and leave now. Anchor at a location I'll show you on the map and don't leave. If any government vessels harass you, tell them you're having engine troubles, and you will leave as soon as the repairs are done. We will start bringing people to you as quickly as we can. Don't leave for any reason!"

"Me be there, mon. Just show me on de map."

I locate an area approximately eighty nautical miles off the shoreline from Cancun. "This will be just the right distance to rendezvous with the sub." After looking at the map, I give further instructions. "Stay at this location and do not move. Two nights from now we should start unloading our first group of people from the sub. I'll flash you three times from the sub at periscope depth. I want you to answer us with two flashes, a pause, and then two more flashes if everything is alright. If there's a problem, don't flash at all."

"Jah, mon. Me be there."

Malik calls over to his crew, "We need to be going now. Me give instructions on de boat." Immediately, he gathers his belongings and heads out the cave entrance.

I find Kurt pounding his chest muttering, "It's my fault. They should have stayed here!"

I grab Kurt's upper arm and look him square in the face, "I promise you we will get them out of there. Right now, you have to get yourself together and just concentrate on getting to Cancun. We need to get this sub out of this cavern and on its way."

Kurt snaps out of his trance. "I know…I know…I'm ready. Let's get on the sub."

Carlos, Kyle, and most of the team are already aboard, making preparations to leave immediately. Steve grabs up his electrical equipment and crawls down through the sub's main hatch.

I yell to Jim up on the dock, "You have to remain behind and monitor the island. Choose a few people to stay with you to help you keep the island secure."

He argues "I can help. Give me a second to grab a few detonators."

"No time. Keep the island safe!"

The remaining people crawl down through the hatch. I snap the main hatch closed sealing it as Kyle prepares to submerge. Our moods are at an all-time low as we take to our stations. The thumping sounds of individuals working to prepare for the rescue echo throughout the sub. Equipment is checked and stowed as the adrenaline pumps through our veins.

"Pull the plug. Flood down to periscope depth," Kyle orders.

The sub rumbles as it sinks below the surface. The decks flood over with sea water.

Kyle again orders his team, "Reverse three knots. Keep the bow plane level."

"Aye, Reverse three knots. Bow planes level." comes the muffled confirmation.

The sub plunges back through the entrance of the cavern without a flaw.

"Helm, left full rudder. Come around to a heading of one-eight-zero."

"Sir, One-eight-zero degrees."

The submarine rocks a little as our heading changes directions. Kyle continues to holler orders, keeping the sub on a direct path to the Yucatan Peninsula. We are on our way to rescue our loved ones from a cruel death. None of us will rest until they are safely out of harm's way.

C H A P T E R 9

RESCUE

The atmosphere on the sub is quite unlike the past few days. All of us are unusually quiet: a feeling of doom hangs over our heads. We can only imagine how our families are feeling. The government has military patrols corralling everyone on the peninsula. Their only hope of survival is on our shoulders. We have to waste two days making our way south of the Dominican Republic and Cuba in order to get to Cancun. It gives us three days to get as many people out of the Cancun area as possible.

We double-check equipment, maps, communicators, scuba gear, and any other important equipment necessary for this mission. These night operations have to be organized to a science and performed flawlessly to get as many people out as possible. Our strategy is to hit a different area each night, continually pulling people out until one hour before dawn. When the submarine reaches its capacity, we will send the sub to rendezvous with the Sea Jewel and off load everyone as quickly as possible into the cargo ship. Malik will take everyone from the nights rescue mission to Belize the next day, until further plans for their accommodations can be made.

Kurt approaches me in the galley. "I can't believe all of this is happening." He hangs his head, then slowly glances up at me. "Do you think we'll find them?"

I look at Kurt's worried face. "You know we'll find them. Carlos and you know that area better than anyone in Cancun. We'll get them all out."

"I just couldn't stand to lose Adrian and Liana; they're my whole life now!" Kurt answers. He is in a frantic state grasping the arm of his chair as if he will break it.

"Don't worry. They're going to be the first ones we're going to take out of there. Catalina and her family too!"

I try my best to cheer Kurt up, even though my own stomach is also tied up in knots. As far as I'm concerned, this sub is not moving fast enough. We have approximately five days to rescue everyone we can, which includes the two days it will take us to get there. We have no way of knowing if the military will move everyone inland or just keep them in concentrated areas on the peninsula. No matter what problems we encounter, all of us will give our lives before letting any of our families face a lottery death squad.

Kyle bends through the hatch as he enters the galley. He looks at both of us as if he can't find the appropriate words. "I'm so sorry this has happened to your families. Secretly, I believe this government has zeroed in on us."

Kurt looks up from the floor and asks, "Why do you think that?"

"I just can't figure out any other reason they chose this area. I'm not sure how it could have happened, but there may be a spy among us. Why else would they target Cancun?"

"The same thought crossed my mind. I just can't believe that someone here would sabotage our operation. It's just not like anyone we picked to turn against us," I say as I rub the hair on my head.

"Stranger things have happened. You can't trust everyone."

Kurt thinks for a second. "We need to search the sub for any communication devices or sabotage equipment. It may be our last chance to find the culprit."

Kyle answers, stepping closer and lowering his voice, "This has to be done carefully. We don't need to tip off this individual. He could sabotage the sub."

It takes me a moment to think of a plan. "Kurt, get Carlos and a few people you trust and have them begin a careful search. They're going to have to be as discrete as possible. We don't need to tip off this traitor."

Kurt gives me an affirmative nod and leaves quickly out the hatch. I begin to search the galley area and surrounding rooms. Kyle slips back to the control room to make a careful search without being obvious. All of us continue to inspect everything without being obvious to the others aboard. Several hours creep by without finding a single piece of evidence or even a slight clue that there may be a spy. If there is someone on the sub supplying information, he is extremely clever. Our first search reveals nothing out of the ordinary. We remain alert and continue to actively search areas we may have missed.

Suddenly, a pounding is heard coming from the main barracks. I race into the room to find Kurt jamming a person up against the wall. His hands clutch the throat of the man who struggles to free himself.

"I think I just found our culprit!" Kurt barks as his grip tightens.

"Don't snap his neck yet. What's he done?"

"Look in his duffle bag. Tell me what ya see!"

I grab up the bag flipping out the contents onto the floor. A device falls out that resembles a communicator. Reaching for the unit, I remind Kurt, "If he's our spy, our whole operation may be compromised."

I pick up the device as the individual attempts to speak, "Pleeeese senor!"

"Let him talk. You have a death grip on his throat."

Kurt lets loose of his throat to give him a second to explain, "It's just a camera. Open the latch senor."

I snap open the clip to see digital electronics and a focal lense. I inspect it closely determining it is indeed a camera. "What are you doing with this? Are you secretly recording images for someone?"

"No No. I brought it along just for fun pictures," the man pleads trying his best to maintain his composure.

"I don't care. It's a security breech!" Kurt wails as he snatches the camera to take a better look. He snaps the power on and glances through the images.

"Your Carlos's friend aren't you?" I ask keeping an eye out for any false moves.

"Si, We are amigos for years." Sweat begins to run down his forehead.

"The images look innocent. We keep the camera until this entire operation is over. I'll check with Carlos to be sure you're checked out. In the meantime stay in this room."

The man nods nervously, slowly sitting down on his bunk.

Kurt and I leave the room to establish the man's identity. I wait until I get far enough away to talk. "You had that guy ready to wet himself. Are you sure the pictures are legit?"

"Yeah, I guess I jumped the gun. It looked like a phone at first. I guess we're all getting paranoid."

"Check with Carlos to be sure. Apologize to the poor guy. He's just helping out."

Kurt leaves to discuss the matter with Carlos. I work my way through the sub, continuing to search for any items that indicate a saboteur. The sub runs flawlessly as we make our way through the Caribbean Sea south of Cuba. Every now and then, sonar records activity above us but without targeting the sub. The

U.S.S. Constellation streams along, invisible to the world around us as Steve keeps the stealth system finely tuned.

We make our way south of Cuba into the Gulf of Mexico, making great time as we approach Cancun, and the Yucatan Peninsula. As we get closer to the peninsula, the activity on our sonar screen increases.

I enter the control room as Kyle gives his next order. "Blow ballast to periscope depth. Bring us around to a heading of zero-eight-five degrees. Sonar, do you record any activity?"

"No sir, not in the last thirty minutes."

"Good. Up periscope."

Kyle grabs the handles of the periscope tightly as it rises to his level. He presses his eyes against the eye piece, slowly rotating the scope in a clockwise direction. He doesn't utter a word as he slowly completes a full circle.

Leaning back from the scope and releasing tension off the grips he announces, "I barely see the coastline of Cancun. I'll take us to within seven miles of the shore line to begin operations tonight. Is everything ready?"

Carlos quickly answers, "We're ready to rock and roll amigos! I know just where to go ashore near my bar. Let's get our families out of there tonight!"

I explain, "We need to start operations at eleven p.m. sharp. All of us will dive from below the sub to the deck and release the skip boats underwater. We'll then head to the surface and get aboard the boats. It should take us no longer than fifteen minutes to get to shore and hide the skip boats. We keep working until six a.m., taking as many people out of the area as possible. Keep your darts loaded and ready to take out anyone who gives us a problem. If there are no questions, then let's get this operation moving!"

"Let's get it done!" Kurt bellows as he turns, making for the hatchway.

Kyle strategically steers the sub, placing it within seven miles of shore near a port outside of Cancun. The clock clicks by the minutes as we ready ourselves for the rescue mission. Tonight is the night all this preparation for the past several months is all about. The intensity of the night is even more compounded by the mere fact that we're rescuing our families.

Eleven p.m. finally arrives and Kurt gives the order, "Let's get to the skip boats. Seal your guns and make sure everyone is carrying enough darts. I want all of our families and friends to be out of Cancun by six a.m."

We don our scuba gear, checking to make sure plenty of air remains in each tank. The pressure gauge on each one reads approximately three-thousand pounds of pressure. Plenty of air for the time we need.

"Grab the weapons, Carlos, and make sure they're sealed. We'll be in a world of hurt without them!" I bark just before pulling my mask over my face. I drop through the dive port, sucking air through my regulator as the water soaks into my wetsuit. The others follow in succession, exiting into the tropical water. One at a time, we make our way around the outside of the sub to the skip boats on the deck. The water sends a chill up my spine as I adjust to the temperature. The boats remain intact on the deck. We take special care releasing them to the surface with a quick pull of the levers. Each boat springs from its resting place bursting out of the water like a cork. I make my way up to one boat and flip myself into it with a quick kick of my flippers.

I quickly glance around for any signs of activity in the area. Boats are moving around in the distance as their lights reflect on the water, but none of them are close. We quickly stow our scuba equipment under the seats that hold our other gear. Three to four divers enter each boat and unseal each engine. The motors start with a hum as the batteries send a pulse of electricity to the plugs. Within minutes, we are quickly heading to the shoreline.

"Keep the boats tight. Everyone stay down and inform the others," Kurt advises the men in the boat next to us.

Fortunately for us, the moon is in its quarter phase, so the night seems darker than usual. Our boats skim quickly along as we approach the beach. I gaze through a pair of night vision goggles checking the shoreline for any people or military personnel. There's no one in sight anywhere in the vicinity. It's time to get ashore and stash the boats.

Carlos previously picked out a spot where the boats can be stashed. An old pier that is slowly breaking apart makes a perfect hiding area. Kurt is the first to spot the pier. "I've got it in sight!" He signals everyone to head to it.

Each boat rams the beach line, placing each one half way up on the sand. Together we pull the boats up under the remaining pier section, being careful not to make unnecessary noises. Carlos instructs his men, "Two of you stay and protect the boats. The rest of you, come with us." He points indiscriminately at his men. "You two will do."

Carlos and Kurt lead the way along sections of palm trees and narrow alleys creeping towards the Casa' de la Parrot. As we get closer to the bar, Carlos notices two or three soldiers in groups guarding the main streets. Our dark camouflage clothing prevents them from spotting us in the dim moon light. Rounding a corner, I catch a glimpse of the bar, noticing that the lights are on. "Keep the faith partners, there's activity inside," I whisper adjusting the sights of the dart gun.

Kurt quietly answers, "I'll bet Catalina, Liana, Adrian, and others are inside, praying for our arrival."

Inching our way around the back end of the bar, we approach the door. Kurt carefully reaches for the door handle staying in a crouched position. He looks back nodding his head affirmatively as the door slowly opens. Kurt, Carlos, and I enter as the others stand guard. A hallway leads up to the main bar area allowing us to get into position for any military intervention. Kurt carefully peers around the corner into the main room. He looks back, holding up three fingers motioning the positions of each guard. He signals us to rush when he drops his finger. He leans against the wall, tilting his head to get a final look.

His drops his finger as we burst through the doorway, taking shots at the three guards. All three victims jerk forward as the darts find their way to their mid-sections. One of them makes an effort to raise his gun. As the drugs quickly take effect, the guards drop to the floor unconscious. At tables closer to the main bar, Adrian, Liana, and about thirty others are startled. They spin around at the sudden collapse of the guards.

Liana responds with intense joy, "Daddy! Thank God you're here!" Kurt quickly places his index finger to his mouth to alert them to stay silent.

Adrian and Liana rush over to us, quietly crying. Gathering everyone together, we make sure the area is secure. One man stands guard outside the backdoor as we prepare to leave.

I ask Adrian. "Where is Catalina?"

"We haven't heard from her since the military came in. She may be held at her parent's home."

"Let's get all of you to the boats. I'll take a few men with me. I'm getting them out of there!"

Adrian quickly urges, "There's about forty people locked in the rooms upstairs."

"Get them down here quickly so we can get everyone out to the sub. Tie these guards up in the storage locker."

Everyone moves swiftly as we prepare to take the first group out of Cancun. Kurt suggests glancing around the room, "Everyone get out of your bright clothing. You don't have to look pretty to make an escape."

I further instruct as I glance out a small window, "Keep together, move quickly, and stay quiet."

We silently flow out of the back door keeping an eye on our surroundings.

Liana reflects frantically as we begin to move, "We have to get the people next door. We can't leave them!"

Kurt pauses, then replies, "All of you wait here, Tony and I will get them. How many guards are there?"

"I've seen only two soldiers."

I propose to Carlos, "Partner, give us ten minutes and head out. Even if we don't make it back."

Adrian grabs us in a hug I will cherish for years. Kurt and I creep back around the side of the house, making our way towards the next building. The windows at the front are well lit, giving us a good view. Both are partially open. Two guards stand near the front door looking back at their captors. A quick glance reveals that the street is vacant. We silently edge up to the window, taking careful aim.

Kurt quietly counts down. "Three, two, one."

Simultaneously, we fire. Darts fling out of the guns with a hiss, sticking into each guard. Both stagger forward and fall as the darts inject the narcotic into their bloodstream. The people inside crouch back as the guards collapse. We quickly enter through the front door, grasping our weapons in front of us. I motion to the captives to stay quiet as we slither through the room. They recognize us and pat us on the backs as we pass.

"The room checks clear," I disclose.

"Keep quiet. Wear only dark cloths and follow us," Kurt whispers to the group.

Quickly we move out the door and make the trek towards the alley. Joining the other group, Carlos and I lead the pack as Kurt scouts ahead of us. Everyone progresses silently, working our way back through the narrow alleys. With every new corner, Kurt maintains his vigilance, signaling us when to move ahead. We make our way towards the pier in a quiet procession. Reaching the beach, Kurt signals with a penlight. The return flash penetrates the darkness, giving us the all clear. Quickly we escort everyone under the pier.

I speak quickly, keeping my voice as low as possible, "Get everyone in the skip boats and get them out of here. The three of you are coming with me."

Kurt urges, "I'm going with you just to make sure you don't pull anything stupid."

Adrian pleads with Kurt as she walks towards a boat, "Please get back quickly! Catalina has to be there. Please get them out!"

"She won't remain here and die at the hands of these son of a bitches!!" I answer her with a quick response. "We'll find them!"

We remain long enough to load everyone on the boats. The rippling tide creates resistance as we thrust each vessel out of the current. Each skip boat creates a flurry of foam as they cast off.

"Let's get moving," I contend. The night air remains serene as we trudge along the sand keeping a low stance against the underbrush. Sprinting across a main drive, we enter the town. Our camouflage outfits help keep us hidden as we work our way through the side streets. Intermittently, a patrol creates a barricade as we traverse side streets remaining in the shadows. From building to building, we crisscross the streets, intensely focused on our surroundings.

"Keep the faith, we're almost there," I disclose quietly as we gaze across a field.

Frogs croak in the distance as we file along the tree line. A misty fog clings around the upper parts of the treetops. The ground is damp from dew that is forming.

'SNAP' We instantly collapse to the ground, detecting a sound in front of us. A slithering creature runs off in the distance. I let out my breath as my finger twitches against the trigger.

Kurt shakes his head. "Getting jumpy, aren't we."

"I about lost my bladder on that one," I confess attempting to repress the tension. "I see their house on the corner. Let's move in."

The house has several lights on inside as well as a few lit on the front porch. As we approach, I notice only one of Catalina's father's cars parked in front. I can only pray they are home and have not been taken to a new location.

Carefully, we creep up to the side of the house keeping a watchful eye out for any movement inside. I slowly peer into a window and notice two guards sitting at the main dining table. They casually drink coffee and engage in a nonchalant debate. We slowly work our way towards the front of the house, glancing through windows. No other people seem to be inside, at least not downstairs.

We inch up to the rear door, entering quietly into a back hallway. I can hear the guards in the next room chatting about the day's activities. Kurt tiptoes down the small hall as I sneak up to the entrance of the dining room. Kurt signals; he's ready. I drop my hand and together we enter from two different doorways. We focus our aim on each guard as we bust into the room. The guards jump; one of them getting to his feet.

"Don't make another move! I promise, it will be your last one ever!" I yell.

Both of them raise their arms up quickly as one answers in a hyper tone, "Please, don't shoot us!"

I poke my gun into the face of one of them asking, "Where is the family who owns this house?"

"I don't know who owns it. When we got here, it was empty. Please don't shoot us!"

Kurt presses the question, "What have you done with the people who live here!"

"I'm telling you! Please, no one is here!"

Kurt looks at me and nods in acceptance to the answer. We both fire our weapons into each guard. They fall forward moaning for a second as the tranquilizer takes effect.

I tap the foot of one to make sure he's out. "Let's search the house. Maybe they're hiding in the basement or attic."

"Let's make it quick. I'll get the others." Kurt responds turning towards the hall.

All of us search the house without finding a soul. The tension I'm feeling begins to engulf me as I become angry and fearful at the same time. All kinds of fear-driven scenarios are going through my mind. I have to find Catalina or die in the process.

"Don't worry pal. We still have a few days to locate her. I'm sure she's close," Kurt attempts to console me.

"Let's get out of here. We'll hit homes on the way back. Maybe someone knows something."

We leave the house feeling frustration from our attempt. We retrace our path. Ahead of us stands a church which appears to have activity going on inside. A few military vehicles are parked outside the front door.

"Partners. It may be risky, but we have to pull these people out." A boldness takes hold of my motivation.

I rush up to a vehicle crouching down behind the bumper. The others follow keeping an eye on the immediate area. I detect music coming from within as I creep a bit closer to get a look inside. A small congregation of people are sitting on benches with military officials standing at two doorways. The timing of our strike will have to be perfect. I look back and signal to Kurt, raising two fingers and pointing to the side door. I tap my watch raising three fingers as a signal in three minutes we attack. He acknowledges with an affirmative gesture. Kurt works his way around to the side door with his teammate. I signal the other two members to follow me. We get in position beside the large front door. I look down at my watch as the seconds click by.

"Get ready. Three, two, one!" We burst through the door firing our darts in a spectacular show of aggression. The guards inside spin around as one or two barbs hit each one. They slump down against the benches. Out of nowhere, a guard bursts through a back door swinging his gun in a wild frenzy. My two compadres open up on him popping him twice, knocking him to the floor before he can get off a shot.

"Outstanding!" I relate to them feeling fairly confident about our hit. A few people gasp as we swing our guns around ready for another intrusion. The people stare at us with wide eyes as we take a count of them.

"There's at least sixty." I determine making a quick count. "You people have been liberated! Just stay quiet and grab only your necessary belongings."

A woman in the back begins to cry chanting prayers with intense emotions. Everyone slowly stands up shuffling along the benches.

"Get rid of your flashy clothing. Wear only dark clothes," Kurt alerts them as we prepare to exit. He points to a few light scarfs and shirts conveying the obvious brightness. The people disrobe the items having radiant colors.

Checking the perimeter before we exit, I look around to check that everyone is ready to move. Kurt and Jose survey the area outside.

"File out everyone. Keep together, and for God's sake, don't make noise," Kurt demands reaching for the door handle to exit.

We empty out the church, leaving the guards to sleep it off. Taking an alley towards the beach, we come across another house with obvious hostages. I motion everyone to stay slouched down in the alley as Kurt and I check out the home. Jose and the others remain on guard.

"This one should be a cinch," Kurt whispers as we near the side door. "I only see one guard in a chair."

As we sneak closer, the door begins to open. We freeze in our tracks with guns aimed. Another guard appears conversing with the one inside, unaware of us. He shuts the door with a chuckle and begins to walk towards us looking at his shoes. As he looks up, Kurt snaps his finger on the trigger expelling a dart into his groin. A surprise look erupts on his face as he falls forward with a grunt.

"I'll bet he didn't expect that one!" I mutter as we file past him to take out the next one.

"We're getting good at this," Kurt snickers in a low tone.

A quick check through the window, indicates only the one guard remains. Ten or twelve people are sitting around the room. "Let me take this one partner." I snap a dart into the chamber. "Open the door slowly at first.' Kurt grabs the door handle creaking it partially open.

"Ya forget something?" The guard inside says. He leans forward and gazes at the widening door.

"Yeah. You forgot this!" I trigger the gun as it inflicts a dart into his thigh. He flinches for a second, then slumps down into the chair. We enter quickly, hushing everyone in the room.

"Don't be alarmed. You're being rescued," I inform them observing their bewilderment.

"There are a few people sleeping upstairs. Should we get them?" An older man yelps in awe of our intrusion.

"I would think so. Someone get them down here in a hurry," Kurt responds looking at me with a smirk on his face.

The older man continues his exchange finally standing up from his seat, "Good, 'cause one of them is my wife!"

Kurt nods his head in disbelief as he grips the banister to the stairway. "That man must have been married for quite a while." He heads up the stairway chuckling to himself.

I feel sorry for the old guy, but it's great to find a bit of humor in this situation. I help him gather his few belongings and encourage him to walk to the door. The others gather as Kurt comes down the stairs followed by six people.

"Is that everyone?"

"Got them all." Kurt looks around, motioning everyone to file out. "Ready when you are."

The street looks clear as I open the door to exit. The guard remains motionless on the ground in front. "Help me drag him inside." I motion a younger man that looks physically fit. We drag the guard past the people and deliver him to a couch inside. "Follow me everyone and stay silent."

Joining the other group in the alley, we continue to hustle towards the beach. The dark alleyways make great cover as we work the group toward our boats. We finally reach the embankment as Kurt signals our comrades under the pier. They return the proper signal allowing us to approach.

Carlos greets us. "We located some more amigos around here. They've already been taken out to the submarine."

We estimate well over three-hundred people have been liberated. It's time to make a run to the Sea Jewel. Everyone quickly climbs into skip boats as we steady them. The engines sputter as we set out to meet the sub. In turn, each boat raises up until the proper speed levels them out against the surf. We race over the waves, leaving the beach behind.

It takes approximately twenty minutes to intercept the Constellation. Everyone files aboard as the crew prepares for a quick run out to the Sea Jewel. The rest of us head back to Cancun for at least two more runs before daylight emerges.

It's three-fifteen in the morning as we pull into the pier area. The boats are hidden as before. A wedge of the moon hangs in the nights sky as we hustle away from the pier.

The areas we concentrate our next rescue efforts on are down the street from the Casa de la Parrot. We pull more of Carlo's and Kurt's friends out of containment, while darting more captors. It's becoming too easy and obvious that no one has alerted them to our operation. We must not have a traitor among us after all. Too many paranoid feelings have created our fears. The question still remains: Why did they pick Cancun?

Our last rescue for the night is close by the pier, as we gather another sixty-five people out of bondage. Everyone climbs into the skip boats for the last load of the night.

I signal Kurt to leave without getting on board. My plan is to stay and find Catalina, no matter what the consequences. I grab my rifle, checking my dart supply, and quickly hustle away from the pier. I look back as three of the five boats leave the shore. I work my way up to the palm tree line and hesitate before crossing the first narrow lane. The street appears quiet enough as I begin to cross to the next set of narrow streets. There is a slight glow in the sky as dawn begins to make its arrival. The only thought on my mind is to get Catalina off of this peninsula as quickly as I can.

Suddenly, I feel an intense burning sensation in my back. I stagger forward as my body begins to feel numb. I drop to my knees, attempting to swing around with my rifle. I notice someone standing over me. I try to move or speak, but my mind begins to fade. Everything goes totally blank.

RESCUE DAY 2

My body and soul feel numb as I struggle to waken from a horrible slumber. I can faintly make out voices around me as I struggle to make sense of my whereabouts. My mind whirls in a fog as I attempt to get my surroundings into synch. I can't determine whether I've been shot or just captured. Vaguely, I can remember collapsing in Cancun while seeking the whereabouts of Catalina.

As I struggle to mentally awaken myself, a familiar voice calls to me. The voice sounds a lot like Adrian. I vaguely make out her words, "Rest now. You're going to be fine." It's a very comforting voice under the circumstances. I strain to listen, but my mind can't handle the pressure as my thoughts fade away.

Suddenly, I feel the presence of someone standing over me. I struggle to open my eyes while focusing on a silhouette. I speak as loudly as I can. "You can kill me, but you can't stop me. I condemn your fucking lottery!!"

A familiar voice answers, "Tony, It's me Kurt. I had to drug you before you got yourself killed. You're on the U.S.S. Constellation with your friends. We got a lot of people out of Cancun last night thanks to you."

I strain to open both eyes, focusing them as I observe Kurt looking down on me. He wears a smile from ear to ear in a smug sort of way.

I fight the raspiness in my voice. "What about Catalina?"

The smile fades from his face. "We haven't found her, but information from a neighbor said they were seen leaving home a few hours before the military landed in Cancun. She could be anywhere."

My mind whirls with thoughts of what may be happening to her. I plan to find her, no matter what the consequences. I shake my head, attempting to clear the cobwebs.

Kurt reads the anguish on my face. "Don't worry, buddy. We'll find her. We still have two nights left."

Even though Kurt makes an attempt, he's not comforting. Only two nights left to look for her, just isn't enough time. "You didn't have to drug my ass. You could have asked me to wait!"

Kurt clears his throat with his arms folded in front of him. He gathers his composure and replies, "I really didn't think you would listen to me last night. I knew you would go out and get yourself killed."

"You're probably right." I can feel a fury building up inside of me. "I'm at total war with these sons of a bitches."

"I'm right there with you buddy. I promise we'll do everything we can do to get Catalina back."

I struggle to a standing position, still feeling groggy from the effects of the drug. My thoughts begin to only focus on finding Catalina. She has to be somewhere in this area. Someone has to know of her whereabouts. Tonight, I'm going to find her or die in the attempt.

Adrian appears in the hatchway carrying coffee and breakfast with a familiar smile on her face. She sets the food tray down and hugs me as if there's no tomorrow. "You guys are the best!"

She whispers to me, "If it wasn't for both of you, my daughter and I would be dead in a few days. I'll never be able to thank you enough."

I stare in her teary eyes replying, "You just did. Seeing the two of you together lifts my spirits!"

Kurt begins to fill me in on missing details. "The Sea Jewel is due to be back soon from Belize, where Malik dropped off the people from last night's rescue. He got the ship moving in record time."

I shake my head to clear the cobwebs. "How will he find us?"

"Malik knows just where to meet us tonight. We picked a location far north of Cancun. The compass coordinates will place him approximately one-hundred nautical miles off the northern tip of the peninsula. Kyle has the coordinates."

I walk over to the mirror and throw a splash of water in my face. I ask, "It may take longer for the sub to reach the Sea Jewel?"

"We can't chance having the Sea Jewel any closer to shore."

The cold water helps clear my head. "You're right."

Kurt elaborates, "In two days, the United Nations is planning to expel gas on the Yucatan Peninsula. Our mission tonight will be tougher than ever. The United Nations military are now aware individuals have been rescued from Cancun. Patrols will be on high alert for any new attempts. It may be the last night we will be able to risk an operation in this whole vicinity. Tonight we have to go ashore further north."

I respond while preparing to shave two days' worth of growth off my face, "It's time to get everything ready for tonight. It eases these feelings of desperation to realize we saved so many people last night." I begin to freshen up as Kurt and Adrian leave through the hatch. A lot of pressure is on our shoulders now.

Several divers are sent outside the sub to evaluate the condition of the skip boats. Each diver has a fresh set of fuel tanks to replace the near empty ones. The attachments holding the boats are checked along with the ability to release each one. Containers on a few of the boats are stocked with medical supplies in case of any emergencies. They are brought to the surface long enough for the engines to be serviced and sealed.

As the skip boats are being serviced, all the guns have to be cleaned and checked for any problems. New darts are prepared with tranquilizer drugs and distributed to everyone involved with tonight's rescue. Scuba tanks are filled making them ready for tonight's rescue.

Steve approaches me in the supply room of the submarine remarking, "Tony! I've got something to show you."

I look up at Steve from my work bench. "I hope it's good news. I don't think I can handle any more bad news today."

Steve replies with a smile, "Oh, it's good news alright. I have been working on something you just may need tonight. Let me show you."

Steve pulls me over to his bunk area and proceeds to pull a large box from beneath his storage cabinet. He quickly unsnaps the lid and hurriedly holds up a flare gun and a flare.

I stare at Steve for a second and sarcastically remark, "You get excited over the simplest of mechanisms."

"No you don't understand. It's a new type of flare I developed. Fire it at night, and I guarantee it will buy you some time."

"Ok, if you say so. We'll take them with us tonight. We can always use all the help we can get. You're coming along with us tonight, so you may want to hold onto one yourself."

Steve thinks for a second remarking, "I made twelve flares with four guns to fire them. Just don't let anyone look directly at them when they launch. I've got dark glasses to hand out just in case."

"Just what kind of flares are these anyways?"

"I used a magnesium core along with a few other elements for an intensified glow that should stop people in their tracks. Like I said, just don't let anybody look directly at them when you light these suckers up."

I look at Steve wondering where he comes up with these ideas. I'm not about to question him on the effectiveness of his flares after all he has done to give our operation its success. Steve and his gadgets have been a Godsend for us.

"Let's make sure everyone has a set of glasses and is aware of the effects."

Steve answers with a grin, "You won't be disappointed. I guarantee it."

I leave Steve, and work my way up to the main control room. Kyle is sitting at his control station, keeping an eye on the sub's operations. He seems to be disturbed by the activities on the radar screen.

I ask as I walk up beside him, "What are you noticing on your screen? It looks like you found a problem I don't want to hear."

Kyle slips off his glasses and gazes at me. "Hey, Tony. I'm seeing a heck of a lot of activity top side. They seem to be all over the area. Our rescues last night have definitely been noticed. Tonight is going to be a bitch."

"We'll just have to get tricky ourselves. Has Malik made any contact?"

"Not yet. We should hear from him soon, though. Belize isn't that far from here."

I consider the scenario for a second and remark, "If Malik doesn't make it back, then we're not going rescue very many people tonight."

"You're right. Only what this sub can hold."

"It just won't do! Malik has to show up. We have a lot of people to get out of there."

"We'll keep a lookout. He may be taking a longer route to get back. I doubt if he wants to get targeted by any military patrols."

"Keep me posted. It won't be long before we need to launch our next mission."

I leave the control room to help finalize the rescue plans with everyone involved. Our plan is to get more people out of this area than we did last night. We can only accomplish this if everything goes perfectly. I also plan to find Catalina or stay on the peninsula until I do. My life is barren without her. She must be close by.

To liberate more hostages tonight, we'll send the skip boats back to the sub as quickly as we can. If we send two boats at a time, it should speed up the process. Our operation tonight has to be flawless. Tomorrow we may be hard pressed to make an attempt.

Kurt, Carlos, Steve, and the rest of the crew are gathering in the storage compartment to discuss tonight's plans. I enter the chamber as a discussion is already brewing. Carlos sits off to the side examining one of Steve's flare guns. He rocks the pistol from side to side studying its mechanisms. "So senor, you say these flares will light up the nights sky like the sun? This I have to see!"

"There is just no way for me to describe the intensity of their glow. I'm telling you, don't look directly into them. Use the glasses!" Steve intensifies his confidence in the flares, "I wish I could demonstrate them, but they'll be seen for miles. Just take my word for it."

"Calm down amigo! I believe you!" Carlos fires back as he tosses the gun back to Steve.

"Let's chill a bit people. We're all on the same side," I insist feeling a bit of ten- sion in the air. I glance around the room looking into the faces of the crew mem- bers who are about to handle another night of uncertainty. Some have looks of confidence, while others wear expressions of doubt. "Last night was a great night. We liberated our families and friends literally from the jaws of death. Tonight and tomorrow night we can free many more people from this hell. All of our plans and hard work over the last several months have reached a climax right now! We need to show these son-of-a-bitches just who they're messing with!"

"It's not what we're doing that's bothering us," Carlos begins swaying back in his chair adjusting it to his hefty frame. "It's the government. Are we just going to keep doing this each time they announce a new area? Amigo, it's only a small amount of people we rescue."

"Ya got a better plan?" I answer aggressively feeling a personal ambush with his question. "These are our people were saving!"

"No. No. You misunderstand me amigo. The government needs to be stopped!" Carlos stammers as he attempts to keep the conversation mellow.

"Sorry Carlos." I sit down swiping my hand through my hair composing myself. "After this assault is over, we're going to slip back in there and send a video feed to the world. We'll let the people decide how tragic this is."

"We can't allow another lottery," Kurt adds reflecting on the people who are still held captive.

I glance around the room noticing the same anxiety in everyone's faces. The room remains quiet for a few seconds as Kurt's statement sinks in.

"After we return to Starpoint, we're going to organize a network." I pause for a second to organize my thoughts. "A network to pressure them to reject another lottery. Even if it takes a massive assault."

"Now you're talking, chief!" Kurt blares out with a bit of an adrenaline rush.

"In the meantime, let's get these flare guns handed out and get a few people out of Dodge." I stand up grabbing a gun from Steve and tossing it back to Carlos. "These may just come in handy."

Suddenly, Kyle announces over the intercom, "The Sea Jewel is making its way to our coordinates. They will be ready for the first load of people we rescue tonight!"

This bit of news revitalizes everyone tremendously, and a cheer echoes throughout the submarine. It's just the kind of news we need to get tonight's operation in high gear. Kyle and his crew maneuver the sub closer to shore as the moment to launch the skip boats draws near. Steve's other three guns and flares are handed out, along with a set of dim field glasses for all. We don't need to blind anyone in the middle of our mission. The glasses will cut down the glare. Everyone dons their scuba gear and double-checks their equipment as the final few minutes click by.

Kyle again announces over the intercom, "The surface appears all clear. Operations can begin. Good luck."

I inform the crew as we gather around the dive port, "We are heading ashore north of Cancun to a town called Boca Iglecia. It's not nearly as populated as Cancun, but info from one of Catalina's rescued neighbors suggests her and her family may be there. We also have a better escape route if trouble shows its ugly head."

The time to exit the submarine arrives, and one by one we exit through the dive port with sealed guns and equipment on our sides. The moisture instantly soaks into my suit as I hit the tropical water. An adjustment to my mask releases a small amount of water seeping in. Diving at night in these crystal clear waters is extraordinary even with just the moonlight as our source. Particles of plankton fluoresce as we disturb the water with our fins.

With a few kicks of my flippers, I follow Kurt around to the deck. The skip boats can be seen clearly as we approach. I detach a flashlight from my leg to find the release lever. The light penetrates the water as I locate the handle, giving it a pull. The boat jettisons to the surface, breaking above the waterline. The other boats pop free as each lever is pulled. I look around as the other divers head up to meet the discharged vessels. Kurt and I climb aboard one boat and prepare to make our run to the beach. Quickly, we shimmy out of our gear fastening it under the seats. We glance around to make sure everyone is in their boats and ready to go. The night air is serene as the waves ripple under the boats in unison.

Within minutes signals appear from the occupants aboard each boat. The engine's crank with a gurgling rumble as we begin to glide through the tropical waters towards the shoreline. The ocean seems calmer than last night, giving us a smooth ride. Kurt gazes through night vision goggles, watching for any movement. We continue moving as the shore line appears. He signals with a flip of his arm, directing us towards an area of palm trees and underbrush. All the boats follow in a direct path toward the beach.

Each one hits the sand driving them up onto shore. The waves clap in behind us as we climb out on the beach and quickly drag them into the underbrush. Several people gather palm branches camouflaging each.

"The town is that way." Kurt indicates with a glance up towards a large palm while pulling off his dive suit. "Hand me my gun. I'll scout ahead while everyone gets ready."

"Gotcha." I toss the weapon to Kurt while getting my own gear together.

The others congregate together in readiness to move on. Grabbing my rifle, we start moving up the sandy dunes. The splashing of the breaking waves dissolves behind us as we snake our way through the brush. Our weapons in hand, darts in each chamber, we continue our excursion toward Boca Iglesia. Working our way through the underbrush, we soon enter the northern end of town. Kurt keeps a careful eye out for any military personnel patrolling the streets.

Carlos whispers to me as he swings a low branch away from his face, "I know this town. Amigo, the main two hotels will be the best place to start. They almost face each other."

I answer keeping my voice as low as possible, "We have to take both of them at the same. Split up into three groups, two from each side and one from the front. We have to time this maneuver so we hit them simultaneously." I glance at my watch, "Spread the word, we strike at one-fifteen."

We creep towards the hotels, noticing military guards outside of each. With darts chambered, we approach the hotels silently in our groups. Kurt and Carlos, each with his own clan, inch towards the hotels from separate side streets. Eight guards will have to be darted simultaneously, four at each hotel.

Steve and I get into position at a church just diagonal to the first hotel. Carlos sends two men as sharpshooters on top of a small building beside the second hotel. They ascend the building by crawling up a drain pipe. A signal soon appears from the rooftop indicating they are in position. The moon casts a shadow across the road as we patiently wait for the seconds to click by. All patrol guards retain their posts as we scope our shots on each one. I keep an eye on my watch as it clicks onto one-fifteen. Darts fly silently from their chambers as eight guards drop quickly from the tranquilizing effects of the drug. The narcotic immediately paralyzes them as expected.

All of us quickly approach the hotels, keeping an eye out for any other guards. I notice Carlos sprinting across the road with his gun held directly in front of him. As we peer through the windows of the hotels, we observe civilians sleeping on the floor in each lobby. Two guards remain inside the main doors of each hotel. Kurt crosses the street, indicating his intentions to enter the other hotel. I return his signal with a flip of my arm.

Carlos grips the door handle twisting it open as I slam it with my foot. The two guards fumble to get a grip on their weapons as we release two more darts. I miss my shot and the dart penetrates the wall. The sentry rips his handgun from his side as I snap another dart into my gun. Instantly I snap the trigger. The dart penetrates his trigger finger before he can squeeze off a round. He drops the weapon with a howl, "Damn!!" He staggers forward to pick up the weapon with his other hand. Carlos snaps another dart into his buttocks. He falls head on into the floor. The impact knocks him out.

"Can't get any luckier than that!" Carlos quips with a chuckle.

The people inside are startled by our quick entry but remain quiet as we move past them. Just as I'm about to enter the stairway, a shot rings out from inside the other hotel. It's a sound that I cringe to hear.

"Make a quick search of the hotel and get everyone into the lobby ready to leave. I'm going to the other hotel to find out what's happened."

Carlos responds, "Don't get yourself shot amigo. I'll be ready!"

I bolt across the street and into the lobby of the other hotel. The first thing I notice is Steve kneeling over a man with civilian clothes on.

"What happened?"

"One of the guards managed to get a shot off as we darted him. It struck this man in the thigh, but with some medical care he should be alright."

"Good. Let's get everyone rounded up and get out of here partner. Have a few people carry him back to the skip boats."

"Got you covered!"

We gather everyone together quickly and begin to exit the hotels. Luckily, the shot seems not to have aroused anyone. We hustle everyone out of the buildings, keeping them silent and together. Two men carry the injured local in a make-shift stretcher. Carlos takes the lead as we quietly maneuver in the darkness. Carefully, we walk through the streets watching at every intersection for patrols. The road winds back towards the beach as we shuffle along. Soon we reach the sand dunes, crossing them in single file toward the awaiting boats. Occasional seagulls fly over us cackling as they glide in formation. The sound of the waves crashing on the seashore resonates along the beach.

The skip boats become our salvation, and we fill nearly all of them with detainees. We are taking more than one-hundred-sixty people out of Boca Iglesia. The boats launch from the shoreline skipping across the waves to safety.

I ask the people in our boat, "Has anyone seen the family of Catalina Delray? Her father is Diago Delray."

One man suggests, "There's more people being held in a warehouse at the south end of town. Maybe they are there."

I inform Kurt, who is busy steering the boat, "This warehouse will become our next target tonight."

The silhouette of the sub soon appears in the shadowy water. We drive the skip boats alongside the sub, latching them to a side rail. People are ecstatic as we help them out of the skip boats and onto the sub. The look outs remain vigilant as everyone is assisted aboard. The last of them step off the boats, giving us a wave as they file down the hatch. Again we launch the skips towards Boca Iglesia at full throttle. The direction this time is south of the town.

Kurt maintains an attentive watch on the beach as we approach. He gazes through night vision binoculars inspecting the tree line. We glide into the beach area with a clear indication that the area is abandoned. The beach has a quick access to the warehouse as described by the Mexican national. An old dirt road is seen across the beach as we drag the boats to a tree line.

"I hope they're here." I comment, feeling a sense of frustration set in. I begin walking towards the road leading the way.

Kurt hurries to my side jamming a fresh magazine into his gun. "We've still got time pal. Somebody will know where she is." He tweaks the sights in anticipation of the next confrontation.

We approach the town, noticing a building ahead of us. It is most likely our next target. We edge along the path, splitting into two groups on each side. Outside along the front of the warehouse are U.N. patrolmen stationed at intervals.

Carlos slithers up beside me. "This is not going to be an easy one, amigo. Look at the location of the warehouse."

"We'll have to surround the building without being noticed. There is only a limited amount of cover for us to work around." Kurt points out keeping his body firmly planted behind a tree.

"There's natural undergrowth. Maybe enough for us to place ourselves around the structure." Carlos offers gazing towards the building.

"Carlos, take your men around the far side of the warehouse. Kurt and the rest of us will slowly make our way around front," I whisper after studying the location for a minute. "You two men work around to the back in case any personnel attempt to flee from the rear. Synchronize your watches to strike together at precisely three-fifty."

Everyone manages to get into their positions without being seen. The patrolmen remain in their locations, casually conversing as we slither into our positions. The seconds click by as we take aim. At exactly three-fifty, our weapons hiss, taking down the guards as neatly as it gets.

The lack of low windows on the building makes it difficult to see the interior. From three directions we storm the building. We distribute ourselves evenly at each door to the interior.

"Our entry will have to be quick and effective!" Kurt mutters to me as we slither up to the door.

"Let's do it partner. We don't have time to waste."

The signal is given, and we rush in through the three entrances. It's fairly dark inside as we enter from the front. From our entrance, two guards are sleeping soundly. We quickly dart them as they sleep. Each group encounters little resistance and the warehouse is secure within two minutes. Men, women, and children line the warehouse floors attempting to sleep in little comfort. Everyone is awakened quietly and told to gather whatever they need and get ready to leave the building. We estimate there are at least two-hundred-seventy people inside we have to get out to the submarine.

Kurt announces attempting to keep his voice low, "We are here to rescue you and get all of you off the peninsula. You must all be as silent as you can when we leave the warehouse. Does anyone know a Catalina Delray or her family?"

A women from the rear answers, "I know them from Cancun."

I excitedly respond to her answer, "Have you seen her or know where they may be?"

"No, I'm sorry. I haven't seen them in weeks."

A great deal of despair comes over me. "Are you sure? Has anyone else seen her?"

A small amount of mumbling can be heard, but nobody responds. People begin to shuffle around picking up their belongings. An uneasiness ripples through my mind as I stand there watching the people assemble. Time is truly running out.

Everyone is rounded up making sure their clothing is dark. We carefully leave the building by the side door passing the downed guards as we go. A few of the detainees give them sharp kicks as we pass. Everyone files down the dirt road making our way towards the beach. The road is narrow, but somehow we manage to stay off the center path. At the end of the large pine trees we find ourselves walking onto the beach. The boats have not been disturbed, and we uncover them and pull them to the breaking waves.

"It's going to take two trips to take everyone out to the sub." Steve suggests, feeling good about the rescue.

"Get half these people out of sight. Keep everyone quiet." I respond sharply, not feeling good about Catalina's disappearance.

The first group climbs aboard the boats, leaving about one-hundred twenty people on the beach for the next trip. Several of us remain, keeping everyone out of sight and hidden along the tree line.

As we wait, I inquire again about Catalina, "Is everyone sure they haven't seen a Catalina Delray?"

No one answers. I am truly becoming tormented by my inability to find her. At least I could hear some good news about her location. Time is running out without even a single clue as to where she could be.

Approximately forty-five minutes roll by before we sight the skip boats. They smack up on the beach and we file down to load them. The crew holds onto the boats as everyone climbs in. I take another glance at the tree line before hopping in myself.

The night is fairly clear, even though the moon is in its darkest phase. The skip boats fly along as we close in on the submarine. We draw closer, and the metallic body of the sub rises from the depths of the ocean. The ballast tanks bubble around the perimeter as it crests out of the ocean. The deck blooms out above water, exposing the hatch.

The skip boats are tied alongside the frame of the sub as we begin unloading people onto the deck. The children and the elderly are carefully taken to the hatch and assisted into the interior of the submarine. We push off from the submarine, making a fast exit to pick up the remaining detainees. I look back, and watch the sub sink back into the sea.

Minutes quickly click by. Our skip boats race toward the shoreline. Kurt watches along the beach with binoculars, making sure our approach remains unnoticed.

"Looks clear. Let's pick them up!" Kurt reports.

"Keep an eye out partner. We better make this fast."

The remaining hostages are quickly loaded, while we hold the boats still in the breaking surf. Each boat races off from shore, when it reaches capacity. I push the final one from shore while jumping into it, leaving the beach behind.

Kurt takes one last look back at the shoreline. "I'm getting hot signals on the night vision specs! There are guards making their way to the beach!"

"Throttle up! They know we just left!" My voice resonates in the tropical air.

Suddenly, snaps from gunfire breaks the still air. A bullet rips through the water near our boat.

"We're being fired on!" Kurt bellows. "Everyone duck down!"

A few people in the boat begin to cry while another bullet hits the water closer to us. The boat streaks steadily along, ripping through the water. The other boats race off far ahead of us.

"Keep your heads down!" Kurt yells another reminder.

I gaze back at the beach as it fades from sight. "We better get these people on the sub quickly!"

In the distance, we notice the silhouette of the submarine. The sight of it quiets everyone within the skip boat. We approach, noticing people already crawling down the hatch. Kurt cuts the motor bringing the boat alongside the sub. We immediately begin helping everyone aboard the deck.

Suddenly Kurt yells out, "There's a gunboat approaching from the south. We've been spotted!"

I look towards Cancun. Bearing down on us very quickly is a U.N. military gunboat.

I roar at the top of my lungs, "Get everyone on board quickly. Everyone with a flare gun get ready to fire them!!"

Lights aboard the gunboat begin flashing, and a tremendous boom can be heard from its deck. People begin panicking on the deck of the sub as an artillery shell from the gunboat rips through the sky above the sub. It explodes upon impact in the ocean just beyond the submarine.

Kurt shouts as he forces everyone but the crew into the sub, "They've fired a warning shot. We have to get out of here now!"

The ultimate sacrifice has to made. I hesitate a second and then command, "Cut loose the skip boats and on my command fire the flares!"

The final liberated individual climbs below the hatch, leaving eight of us on the deck as the gunboat bears down on us. "Get ready to fire and put those dark glasses on!"

The eight of us pop on the glasses as Steve, Carlos, and two others aim the flare guns at the approaching gunboat.

"Fire now! Get in the sub!"

The flares streak skywards toward the gunboat, giving off an incredibly fierce glow that increases in intensity as the seconds click by. The eight of us jump down through the hatch sliding down the ladder rails. The glow of the flares blind the individuals on the gunboat as the intensity increases with every second.

Spinning the hatch closed I yell, "Get us down and out of here!"

The sub shakes and rumbles as it sinks out of sight of the military boat. It rocks side to side as it picks up momentum, making a break for the deep blue sea.

WHAM WHAM

Another explosion rocks the sub. The floor we stand on begins to angle downward as the sub dives deeper. We stare at the metallic ceiling in fear, waiting for another round. A minute passes as we anticipate another explosion. The sub accelerates without a sound from above.

I quickly make my way to the control room where Kyle is bellowing orders to his crew. "All ahead full. Bubble down ten more degrees!"

I look at Kyle and cringe inside as I suggest, "Well, that's the end of our operation. The skip boats are history."

He looks at me with a slightly worn expression on his face. "We did real good. We got a lot of people out of there that would have died otherwise. We did it without suffering any casualties. Steve's flares saved our asse's!"

I nod, leaving the control room. I realize that Catalina is doomed to die. I can do nothing to stop it. I work my way back to the engine area of the sub where I can be alone with my thoughts. I would have stayed on the peninsula and died trying to find her. If only I could continue to search one more night. I have reached one of the lowest points in my life. Nothing will ever be the same.

Later that night we pull alongside the Sea Jewel and unload the remaining people. In all, we rescued over thirteen-hundred people from the death squad of this sick lottery. Kurt instructs Malik to take all the people to Belize and return to Jamaica to wait for our instructions. We will make contact later and inform him of our next plan. As for everyone on the submarine, our mission on the Yucatan peninsula is not quite over. We still have more work to accomplish.

C H A P T E R 11

THE AFTERMATH

The following day leaves us feeling like the day of a funeral. All of us realize our operation has completely ended. Kyle and his crew position the submarine quite a ways off the Yucatan Peninsula while we await the lottery's execution orders. At noon time tomorrow the gases are due to be released in predetermined areas on the peninsula. The gas is said to dissipate within hours after having suffocated everyone in its path and is known to be lethal for only a few hours. Death is inescapable for anyone who breathes it. Emotionally, everyone is ready to crumble. We all know what is happening on the peninsula and can do nothing more to stop it.

Several of us plan to go ashore a day or two after the gas is released to produce a video feed of the devastation. We have to show the world what is happening here. The media will not be allowed to record or film the mass killings. We plan to secretly sneak ashore and send a video feed of the evidence. People around the world will have to witness this cruelty for themselves.

Everyone on board knows the torment I'm going through. All of them do their best to help ease my mind and keep me occupied. It is hopeless though. I have a hate in me towards the governing party of the United Nations that can't be matched. I plan to seek total revenge and justice for this cancer they call a lottery. They have personally taken and will murder the only woman I have truly loved in my life. I wish for their fate to be a thousand times worse than the fate they will deliver to the people of the Yucatan Peninsula. I think of going ashore and taking a breath of this gas myself, but I will do better by staying alive and fighting against this insanity.

Tomorrow, the U.N. will massacre more people in one day than any government or ruling power has since the dawn of time. It's definitely a low point for humanity. No one should die so needlessly and tragically. I'm destined from this day forward to rid the planet of the people who thought up, developed, and influenced this lottery. We need to replace these people with men and women that respect humanity and live their lives to uphold it. I know the original concept of the U.N. has always been respectable. I try to hold accountable only the governing men and women for this lottery and not the United Nations government itself.

Two tragic days pass us by as we pray for the people on the peninsula. The sub remains steady while we hope for the best, but expect the worst. We wait for an opportunity to don our scuba gear and sneak onto the peninsula near Cancun. It may be the only chance we have to evaluate the outcome.

A radio message from the president breaks onto the airwaves, "As your president, I am saddened to bring you this message. The people of the Yucatan peninsula have made the ultimate sacrifice by giving their lives to help with the plight we face today. We pray that their peaceful passing will help feed the many starving people around the world. As our population decreases more food can be offered to feed the masses. I have initiated this lottery only as a last resort to save many more people in the future. This lottery will only continue until we reach a balance between food production and population. I pray with you for the people we have sacrificed. May God help us in these dark days.

"They haven't seen dark days yet." Kurt mutters as he snaps the radio off.

"I swear as I stand before you, there won't be another lottery!" I insist looking at the floor in disgust.

Kyle and his crew maneuver the submarine into an area just north of Punta Cancun. The activity on scope above us is, surprisingly, getting quieter. Larger vessels we have recorded days before have left. We imagine they have abandoned the area in fear of inhaling the fumes themselves when the gases were released. Kyle approaches the conning tower and peers through the periscope. He makes a complete circle before stepping back.

"Down periscope. The area looks unusually quiet. It's about two hours before daybreak, so if you guys are going to go, then now is the time. Just make it back quickly," he remarks in a somber tone.

"We're only going to record a quick feed. I don't think I can stand to see too much of it. I promise it will be a quick trip," I answer looking at the scope making sure the surface activity is vacant.

"Just make it back in one piece. That goes for all of you!"

Four of us will make the journey to record the events that have transpired in the area. Kurt, Carlos, Steve and I begin to get into our gear. Steve gathers together all the necessary video equipment we need. Carlos grabs the dart guns, along with darts in case of any encounters with the military. It's not a trip I'm looking forward to, but one that is necessary in order to topple this government.

"Is the video feed working?" I question Steve as he fiddles with the controls.

"Yeah, fine. We have to keep it sealed. Any water will fry it."

"Seal it up tight, then. Let's not waste our time!" I bark

Kurt pulls me aside. "Are you sure your up to this? Someone else can go."

"Not on your life, partner. I need to see it for myself."

"Lighten up on Steve then. He feels your pain."

"Your right. I'll make it up to him."

I walk over to Steve as he seals the camera for the underwater journey. "Steve, I didn't mean to come off as an ass. Tell me about this camera of yours. Will it broadcast a feed?"

He looks up expressing a slight smile. "The camera gear we cart is fairly sophisticated. The video feed will be automatically sent to a recording unit aboard the Constellation. It will be sent by satellite to many broadcast news networks around the world. We plan on a two- or three-hour delay of our broadcast in order for us to escape the area. If anything happens to us, the recorded material will still be safe. A permanent chronicle will get through to the networks."

"You amaze me brother. Wish I had your intelligence."

His smile broadens as he exclaims, "I'm no more intelligent than you. I just find all this science real interesting."

"Well, whatever it is, keep it up."

The four of us double-check all the equipment and prepare to dive. Adrian and Liana enter the compartment to see us off. Tears flow from the two of them as we approach the hatch in preparation for our dive.

Adrian pleads with anxiety written all over her face, "Please don't go ashore if you detect any gas. I'd go insane if anything happens to any of you!"

Kurt holds her tight answering, "You know I'm going to watch these guys like a hawk. Nothing is going to happen to us. If even a hint of the gas remains, we will head right back to the sub."

She embraces me doing her best to hold back tears. "Keep them safe. Remember, your torment is also ours."

Adrian and Liana grab Steve and Carlos in a quick hug as Kurt and I mount the dive platform. We enter the water through the dive hatch, passing the camera and equipment down. Steve and Carlos follow us as they appear out of the bottom of the sub. We gather in a circle as Kurt points in the proper direction. Side by side, we head out towards the beach.

The clarity of the crystal-clear water can't be matched. Even at daybreak, the marine environment is amazing. The visibility is perfect as we make our way past colorful reefs with multitudes of tropical fish. Heads of colorful coral project up from the bottom. An occasional stingray flutters by as we make our way toward the beach at Playalas Perlas in Cancun. Utilizing an underwater compass, we swim along the reefs until we spot pillars from a pier.

Carefully, we rise to the ocean's surface next to a pillar. Our heads bob out of the water as we observe the beach and the surrounding area. The entire area appears deserted.

I pull out my mouthpiece, whispering to the others, "Let's move in." Carlos suggests, "Stay under the pier amigos."

We creep slowly from pillar to pillar, toward the beach keeping our bodies submerged. Upon reaching the sand beneath the pier, we make a quick dash to the first pillar underneath the boardwalk. The air seems clean without any scent of the gas. Around the beach lay a few dozen dead seagulls. Quickly, all of us make a quick sprint across the beach to a boat house just beside the pier. A large unused bait container provides us a place to stow our scuba equipment.

"Let's go towards Av. Bonampak. It's a road I've taken that runs directly into town," Carlos suggests in a low voice. He remains spooked by the sight of dead birds.

"Let's just get in, do our video, and get out! I don't like this quietness. It disturbs me! Even the birds are silent," Kurt answers in an uneasy tone.

"They don't have to monitor the area or keep anyone from escaping. The son of a bitches have done their dirty work and are probably afraid to get gassed themselves." My cynical remark receives an affirmative nod from all three.

Kurt hesitates for a second as he gazes around the area, "Let's get this done before we become their next victims. I'm telling you; I don't like the feeling here."

As we quietly make our way along the road, we pass more dead birds and animals. The morning sun is beginning to show brightly, giving the horizon a purplish hue. It makes our ability to stay hidden much more difficult. I have to admit, the atmosphere, along with the sightings of dead animals, gives me an uneasy feeling. Even though we are able to breath without a problem, remnants of the gas could still be lethal.

As we pass into the first main intersection, the sight before my eyes is one I will never forget. People are lying about in the streets and walkways dead from the effects of the gas. Some are in sitting positions hugging a loved one, while some are sprawled out as if they died running. Mothers are clutching children; couples huddled together against buildings as the gas seeped into their lungs, taking with it their life. Lovers lay against each other in a final embrace.

I drop to my knees as a sudden feeling of weakness comes over me. I can't believe what I'm witnessing. Somewhere Catalina and her family are heaped together in the same fashion. Tears roll down my face as I stare at the grotesque sight. I have been in combat and war for years, but I have never seen such a horrifying sight as this one. Kurt, Carlos, and Steve remain motionless in a state of shock as they gaze out at the bodies.

I slowly stand up regaining a little composure. "Steve, turn on the video feed and let's show the world what these sons of bitches have done!"

Steve fumbles with the camera and replies in a chocking voice, "This is worse than I could ever have imagined! Let me get this video on before I lose my stomach."

Steve turns on the camera and begins to scan over the people who lay before us. He staggers several times as the view through the lens only gets worse. He nervously zooms in on mothers and children, trying to stop from shaking as he does so. The camera works its magic as it sends video feed back to the sub, recording everything we are witnessing. Carlos, Kurt, and I watch for any movements around the area as Steve records.

Twenty minutes of recording time is all we need to demonstrate to the world how brutal this lottery is. We finish recording as Steve lowers the camera wiping a tear away from his eyes.

I break the silence suggesting, "Let's get back to the submarine before we become their next target."

Carlos glances back at me in a panicky voice, "I've seen more than I can stand amigo. Let's get out of here!"

Steve silently turns off the video as we walk slowly away from the area. Taking the same path along Av. Bonampak, we make our way back towards the beach. After witnessing so many people spread in haphazard cruelty, the silent walk back appears to take longer than the hike into town. Finally, our trudging footsteps brings us back to the boathouse. Our scuba gear remains untouched. The waves breaking on the shoreline is the only distinct sound. The normal chatter of sea gulls, the distant laughing of children playing, the blaring of horn traffic, sounds you took for granted until they are missing. The area is left with an eerie quietness except for the hissing noise of the breaking waves.

As we head down toward the shoreline along the pier, a whirling sound can be heard coming from the south end of Cancun. Surveying the landscape, we observe a military helicopter heading our way. Gun turrets stand out from its sides as it closes on our position. It's not a friendly sight to behold as we scamper for the shoreline.

Kurt howls, "I think they've spotted us! Stay along the pillars for cover. Get as deep underwater as you can."

All four of us sling on our gear as the helicopter approaches. We barely make it to the first pillar before the helicopter hovers above us. Gazing up through the crystal water, we see the guns of the helicopter aiming down upon us. We paddle ferociously to get behind the pillars. Suddenly, the water around us becomes frenzied as bullets rip through, striking the objects around us. Chunks of rock material from the pillar in front of us come tumbling down. We have to make an aggressive swim to the ocean depths.

The pier pillars act as barriers, keeping us from being chopped to pieces. The clarity of the water only hinders our retreat as we dodge bullets from pillar to pillar. They continue firing their weapons as they maneuver to get a perfect shot. Pushing with all our might, we paddle in an attempt to reach deeper water. As we make a break for another pillar, a bullet zips by my head, striking Steve in the right leg. He arches grabbing his thigh while cringing in pain. His body whirls around from the impact. Kurt and I latch onto him from each side pulling him quickly towards the ocean depths. Blood streams from his injury as he becomes limp from the pain. We persist in our efforts using the reef as camouflage in our escape. Slight glimpses of the helicopter attempting to maneuver above us, intensify our struggle. We press on as the chopper loses sight of us. Steve's blood trail may give them the idea we are dead.

As the helicopter fades from sight, we dive deeper into the depths of the ocean. Steve is in obvious pain and growing weaker as we pull him along. The blood continues to flow from the wound. A new problem becomes obvious. Steve's blood trail is certain to attract sharks from the area. Reaching an area deeply surrounded by a reef, we triage Steve's leg. The bullet passed through the outer section of his right thigh, causing a section of the skin and muscle to be torn back. Grabbing the camera from Steve, I unlace the strapping from it. We tie it as a temporary tourniquet to slow down the bleeding. The bleeding eases as I tighten it. Taking a quick look at my compass, we continue moving toward the area harboring the submarine.

Carlos abruptly begins banging his scuba tank in an attempt to get our attention. I glance at the area he indicates. Coming up from behind us about forty to fifty feet back are three tiger sharks following the blood trail. The sub is not close enough to reach before tangling with them. Kurt holds out a dart gun motioning his intentions to drug them. There is no proof the drug in the darts will have any effect on sharks. The velocity of the darts may not even travel through water. We have no other choice but to use them in our defense.

The sharks maneuver closer to us winding back and forth as they sense blood in the area. Kurt takes aim, while waiting for the first one to make its attack. One shark sways making a closer move in our direction, coming within ten feet of us. Kurt establishes a careful aim, quickly releasing two darts that strike its side. Within thirty seconds the shark begins to flinch. With a kick of its tail, the darted shark swims by. The other two sharks circle at a greater distance, waiting for a chance to charge. The drugged shark begins to slow down as its momentum lags. All of us stand our ground waiting for the effects to show.

The drug is working! The creature begins a nosedive to the bottom. Kurt takes aim on another shark as it challenges our position. It attempts to charge forward with its dark lifeless eyes upon us. He manages to fire three darts quickly into its midsection. It flinches as the needles penetrate its tough hide. It uses a quick burst of power to turn. The drug quickly pumps through its blood stream, slowing its motion. Both sharks become motionless, resting at the ocean's bottom.

The last shark begins a direct path towards us. It rolls its eerie black eyes back as it lunges forward towards Kurt with its mouth wide open. Its multiple rows of teeth appear like knives. He snaps off two shots, hitting the shark directly in its mouth. It brushes him as it makes a pass; knocking Kurt aside. He fires one more dart into its tail. The shark slows as it attempts to turn. It moves towards us, but slowly sinks in an effortless attempt.

We grab onto Steve and again paddle forward towards the sub. Maneuvering around coral heads and reef sections, all of us maintain a vigilant lookout for the submarine. Like a miracle, it appears in the distance waiting for our arrival. We kick our way to the hatch and get Steve through the opening. The rest of us crawl through, thanking our lucky stars we made it.

Steve is hustled back to the rear section of the sub where they initiate medical treatment on his leg. The injury has substantially torn back a section of his thigh.

The muscle and tissue will have to be sewn back together and given the proper time to heal. It's a close call for Steve and all of us.

Kyle comes down from the control room, entering through the hallway hatch. He remarks, "You guys made history today! The signal came through fine. We recorded it without a hitch. The signal will go out in about twenty minutes by satellite. The whole world will bear witness to the madness this lottery has caused. I could hardly stomach what I saw from your video feed."

I shook my head back and forth at Kyle, "You can't imagine how bad it is unless you see it for yourself. It's a scene I 'll never forget!"

"Just the silence gave me the jitters. Everything we came across was dead," Kurt adds with a shudder.

Kyle recaps, "Well, our work here is done. It's time to regroup and plan our next step."

Kurt throws his arm across my shoulder. "Tony, I'm sorry to bring up a terrible subject, but I'm so sorry we could't find Catalina in time. She will always be in our thoughts and prayers."

I look at Kurt and the others and can see they are hurting almost as much as I am. It suddenly becomes clear that all hope is now gone: my Catalina is dead. An emotional wave comes over me, but I hold back my feelings. I nod without saying a word. All I can do now is avenge her death.

Kyle senses the intensity of the moment and changes the subject, "You guys get some rest. I'm going to take this sewer pipe of a sub and head back to our island. I think we all need a good rest."

With the first rescue mission behind us now, it's time to recover and heal from all we have been through. The stealth system is working great, so there's little chance of being spotted as we head out to sea. The last few days have yielded many victories, and at the same time we suffered many tragic loses. I have to try my best to continue and not fold under the tragic loss in my life.

Kyle maneuvers the U.S.S. Constellation towards the Caribbean. Everyone on board remains determined to retaliate, with all their energy, against this government. We make a pact that another lottery will never happen. Kyle sets a heading back to our island in order to make plans to attack the government directly. We will unleash revenge for what the United Nations government has done on the Yucatan Peninsula.

C H A P T E R   12

MIRACLE SHIP

Our trip back to Starpoint Island is uneventful. All I want to do is sleep and try to regain some mental strength. A good part of my emotional state is depression. I wish I could just sleep, then awaken with everything restored as it was before. The images from the last few days, especially the last day on the peninsula, keeps appearing in my nightmares. I begin to see Catalina lifeless in the middle of all those people that were killed. It's truly beginning to tear me apart. I should have had the chance to just stay on the peninsula and face the same death as her.

Kyle sounds the all clear as we enter the cavern and begin to surface within it. He orders, "All stop. Blow the main ballast tanks dry. We've made it home."

We break the surface within the cavern. Carlos opens the main hatch releasing us one-by-one onto the main deck of the sub. "Will you look at this, amigos!"

On the surface ledge of the cavern, Jim and the people we left behind begin to cheer us as we walk across the deck. One of them has hung a banner that reads, 'Long live the crews of the miracle ship and the ghost sub'. It doesn't make sense, but we will soon find out what it represents. I have to admit it raises my spirits a great deal to get back to Starpoint. We really appreciate this great reception. The interior of the cavern is surely a sight for sore eyes. A newer gang plank has been made in our absence and is lowered down to the deck of the sub.

Steve is carefully hoisted out of the sub onto the deck. We all applaud him as he is placed onto a homemade stretcher. Steve's marvelous ingenuity with stealth systems got us back to the island and kept us from being destroyed.

"Don't applaud me. Applaud the lives of the people we rescued. It's worth every bit of the pain," he remarks as we take him into the back of the cavern.

"Get better kid. I'm going to need you to keep this stealth system of yours up and running," Kyle answers him.

"Just let me know if it acts up."

He's taken by stretcher into a section of the cavern where he can be treated for his wounds.

Adrian informs us, "It will take time for his thigh to heal before he can get around on his own. He's had quite a bit of trauma to it."

As we walk back toward the submarine, Jim Turner excitedly informs us, "The rescue mission has hit the airways. You guys are considered conquering heroes among everyone that isn't in the military. The Spanish speaking people are calling Malik's ship the 'Milagro Barco' or 'Miracle Ship'. They're calling the sub the "Fantasma Submarino" or 'Ghost Submarine'."

"What else are they saying?" Kyle asks with a degree of interest.

"The mission is being talked about worldwide. They're reporting that your rescue mission saved countless lives in the wake of the government's inhumane release of the poisonous gas on civilians. They also report how humane the rescue was to use drug tranquilizers instead of bullets. They report how the submarine is considered a ghost in the water: disappearing in a flash, leaving no trace."

"Our exploits are planting the seeds for a worldwide rebellion against the United Nations. The media is now pumping this rebellion." I remark feeling more satisfied regarding our operation.

Jim continues to fill us in with details. "The footage you videotaped on the peninsula has also hit the networks. The feedback we are receiving is as good as we could ever hope for. People are devastated around the world, calling this the worst tragedy of the century. Riots are taking place around the world with more intensity than when the lottery was first announced. The military police are retreating and being overrun in some parts of the world."

"It's time to discuss and incorporate our next set of plans for the fall of this government. We need to network with key people in a multitude of areas across the globe." My mind swirls with plans of rebellion. "We have to keep the media hedged against them."

Kyle walks up and hears the conversation. "Be careful what you wish for. It might come true."

"You think we're going overboard? You saw what those bastard's did in Mexico."

"No. I'm just saying that a failure of government will cause chaos."

"Chaos is what we have now, partner. I don't think it can get any worse." Kyle has a point. we need to handle our affairs carefully. "I realize what you're saying. It's not the government I'm after, it's the few men implementing this lottery. Stanovich for certain."

Kyle backs up his statement, "If we do this properly, we can destroy their credibility and run them out of the government."

"I believe we're half way there. The news reports support that," Kurt adds listening to our exchange.

"These networks will spread anti-lottery sentiment everywhere. Hopefully, causing the downfall of these officials. The world can't afford another lottery. Blameless civilians are the only people suffering and dying." I restate our mission.

"I don't see it any other way," Kyle implies stroking his beard in deep thought.

"As long as the main government is spared, I'll stay involved. I agree, a few rotten apples have spoiled the batch."

"Then let's get to it." I wrap up our disagreement to begin making contacts. Several of us begin making connections with individuals we trust. Our communications utilize a satellite linking system that can't be traced back to us. Steve set this link up before we left for the Yucatan Peninsula in case of emergencies.

Kurt locates Thomas Chess, our buddy who lost his leg in the navy. He's now living in Canada. He responds over the link, "I'm more than happy to start up a network in Canada. I will stay in communication while establishing my own trusted group that resists the government. Keep me posted."

More people are contacted in Mexico, the United States, Germany, Australia, Europe, Japan, South America, India and France. They are all eager to secretly branch out with their own groups. These networks will become the base for a unified global underground supporting a revolt against the men running the United Nations.

I continue to stay busy, keeping my mind off my lost love. It's the only way I can survive. I use the satellite link to make contacts with a few more old navy buddies in the United States. They are just as eager to unite with us and branch out their own assemblages.

The satellite link is our only communication with the outside world. Any trace attempted will just be scrambled and diverted around the world. This link is just used for the most important communications. Our security depends on it.

A day-and-a-half slips by while most of us do our best to stay busy. Radio and media reports keep us up to date on everything that is going on in the world. The government has us tagged as the most sought-after fugitives on the planet. There are security forces looking for us in all ports and waterways. They want to shut our operation down.

Descriptions of Malik's ship are totally erroneous from the reports we receive. People involved are giving wrong descriptions to help us evade capture. None of the reports described it as a colorful Jamaican spectacle on the water. I just hope Malik and his crew made it back to Jamaica without problems. We are hoping to hear from them soon.

The government knows which submarine we are using, but has little information about the stealth system we use to camouflage it. Occasionally, a news report announces a possible sighting of the sub. One such report had us sighted in the Indian Ocean, just west of Australia. They continue to refer to it as the 'Ghost Submarine' and wonder about our location.

Kurt takes the position as lookout at the upper cave entrance when he spots a smaller craft approaching. He relays the sighting to us through an electronic sound and signal device. Upon hearing the signal, I clamber up through the cave to find Kurt starring off into the distance.

"Have we got visitors? What do you see?"

"Take a look out to the Northeast." He points off into the distance.

Climbing up to his position, I notice a smaller boat with twelve to fifteen people on board. They are speeding their way around the island tip, heading for the interior of the lagoon. Adrian appears, bringing out a pair of binoculars for us.

"Here guys. See if these help."

I hold the binoculars up to my eyes adjusting the focus. Scanning the occupants in the boat, I can see that our visitors are recognizable.

"It's Malik. Let's get down there and help them out," I announce loudly handing the binoculars to Kurt.

We make our way down through a pathway and quickly run onto the beach. As we get closer to the approaching boat, it appears as if everyone on board is in good spirits.

"You guys are a sight for sore eyes. How did the trip back go?" Kurt yells out to them.

Malik smiles his usual way answering, "We did real good, mon. Me got the people off the ship in Belize. We head back to Jamaica. Things go fine, until we land in Jamaica. Me tie the Sea Jewel up and make town for a feast. When we return, military police search the Sea Jewel. All of us get out of there. Me not sure if they think the Sea Jewel used in the rescue. We got this boat and head here fast, mon."

They throw out the anchor to us and begin to disembark. Malik hops onto shore as the boat rocks a bit from the waves. He steadies himself coming up beside me.

I pat Malik on the shoulder, "Well Malik, they're not going to find you here. Don't worry about the Sea Jewel. When we need it, we'll get it. We've got bigger plans ahead of us."

Malik grins and starts walking with me back towards the upper cave entrance. I have to let Malik know the bad news. It's better if I tell him, rather than have him hear it from the others. I know that Catalina and Malik had a little kinship between them, especially after the snake incident he pulled on her.

We walk him ahead of the others. "Malik, I have to tell you some bad news. We could't find Catalina or her family. None of them have been seen and as far as we know, they have been killed on the peninsula."

Malik's manner suddenly changes. He gasps with a look of terror, "No, mon! No! I'm sorry, Tony!"

I nod slightly, fighting back a tear as we slowly walk toward the cave entrance. The two of us become silent in our own thoughts for the next several minutes.

As we reach the mouth of the cave, Malik motions for a person behind us to come forward. He discretely introduces, "Tony, me waan yah to meet sum'ady special. Me find har when me tak de laas group to Belize. She be wit de laas group of people yah rescued."

A young lady with jet black hair and a beautiful complexion comes up shyly behind us. She looks up at me with a tear running down her right cheek.

"Tony, me waan yah to meet Juanita," Malik announces.

She wraps her arms around me and begins crying, "My life was going to be taken from me until all of you came to my rescue. I owe you my life!"

I whisper to her, "This lottery should never have happened. I just wish we had more time to get more people out. You don't know how much you lift my spirits."

"All of you are very special!" She answers.

It's great to see Malik with a woman like Juanita. It's just the kind of romance Malik needs. I wish Catalina could be here to see the two of them. We walk inside the cave entrance and work our way down into the cavern. We begin to reminisce about the operation over the last several weeks, when a broadcast over the radio captures our attention.

A news reporter announces, "The United Nations military force has issued a bulletin regarding the missing submarine, U.S.S. Constellation. Any person supplying information leading to the capture of individuals responsible for its hijacking will be rewarded. The government has placed a five hundred-thousand dollar bounty for this intelligence. Any citizen who comes forward will remain anonymous. The government will take all measures for security for anyone who comes forward. In related news, individuals aboard a cargo ship with Jamaican registry are also being sought in connection with the resent rescue of detained individuals from Mexico. The government released a document today issuing arrest mandates for the owners of this vessel. Citizens are encouraged to come forward if they have knowledge of the whereabouts of owners of a ship named The Sea Jewel. The cargo ship was found abandoned in Jamaica."

"My God, they're onto us!" Kurt yells as he drops a cup of coffee on the rocky surface.

"No mon! They have me ship!" Malik cries out in a fit of hostility. He drops his head down onto his hands. "Me be out of business now!"

"Malik, don't fret, partner. There's no way they can find us. By the time we organize a rebellion, your ship will be decorated with ribbons." My mood takes a drastic turn. Malik sits up, hoping I'll have some good news. "It won't be long before they know who most of us are. If we organize successfully, we can unseat these prima donnas. Half the world is ready to fight now. Who wants to live in a world where every three months you have to worry if you're the next target?"

"I don't mind having a price on my head! Let the bastards try and find us!" Carlos boasts, adding to my spiel. "If we never embraced this campaign, amigos, all of our asse's would be dead right now! I personally want to rip their hearts out!"

"Carlos knows what I'm talking about. Let's get busy and stop these maggots!" A bit of adrenalin pumps through my veins in response to the radio broadcast. "Who's wives and children will it be in three months from now? Are you with me?"

A thundering response echoes off the rock walls, "Yeah! Yeah!"

Fortunately for us, no one really know of our whereabouts, but I believe most people would reject this offer. People hail us as heroes. Banners are being flown that read, 'Long life to the crew of the Miracle Ship and the crew of the Ghost Sub'. I know the day is coming soon that the United Nations will wish they never created such a lottery.

Contacts we've made are doing a stupendous job of gathering people together. Thomas Chess in Canada has gone so far as to create a hidden location from which to operate. Other contacts in various other parts of the world are organizing and preparing for a revolution if necessary. People we reach in France and Spain are offering ships, submarines, and even airplanes if they are required. The outpour of support is incredible. Most people are petrified that the next grid the government's lottery will select, will include them.

Rioting in various parts of the world are increasing in magnitude and intensity. Government military personnel in certain areas are being overrun. Reports flowing in from the media expound on patrols laying down their weapons and joining the resistance. Some retreat, unable to subdue the onslaught. The U.N. is becoming strained under the pressure of the anti-sentiment. They want to shut us down now more than ever.

Jordan Stanvich is being ridiculed for his support of the lottery. He and his followers reject this skepticism. He explains in a special telecast, "This lottery, although painful to watch, is going to produce a world without starvation and hunger. The sacrifices of a few will save the lives of many as our dwindling food supplies are able to produce larger portions for each individual, ultimately establishing a better world in the future. I stand by my convictions, and move to keep this lottery intact and fight any resistance."

I wonder how this mad man has ever been elevated to a level of such power. Although history is full of men that resemble him, the values of the world can't afford such a man to lead the world into the future. When will this government ever learn from the mistakes of the past? It's time to eliminate these men from power and replace them with men and women who will uphold the values and freedoms of humanity.

Starpoint Island is quickly becoming the central pivot point for the underground resistance around the world. We can't afford mistakes as our networks grow. Our location has to be kept secret at all costs. Steve's stealth system has to be monitored around the clock. Any problems or power failures can be disastrous. Steve is beginning to get around on a crutch as his leg wound heals. He configures system updates and adjustments as necessary to keep the system running at peak performance.

To keep our security tight on the island, the smaller boats and equipment are camouflaged in case of aerial searches. Everything is hidden from sight. Military search vessels continue to patrol everywhere, looking for the U.S.S. Constellation.

After the discussion concludes, I decide to spend few hours fishing. It's an attempt to get my mind off of Catalina. The endeavor is futile though, my mind reels with thoughts about her. It will take a long time to get over her.

Kurt approaches me as I throw my line off of a small rock jetty. He yells out, "Tony, have you caught us dinner yet?"

I grin a bit, knowing how Kurt loves seafood. "Take a look at the stringer. There have to be four or five nice Sheepshead on there. I know you didn't come all the way down here just to look at my fish."

"You're right." He jumps down from a rock ledge to get closer. "I just talked with Carlos. When this mess is all over with, he wants both of us to share in the Casa' de la Parrot bar. No hurry on a decision. Just wants us to know we are considered family."

"Tell him I appreciate the offer, and I'll think about it. But right now, I just have to get my head together."

Kurt scratches his head answering, "I know what you mean buddy. All of us are here for you. When you finish fishing, I'll have a drink of rum waiting for you."

"Thanks partner. I'll need one."

He fidgets, looking out on the horizon. "If you need to talk, I'm here if you need me," Kurt stammers, feeling a bit uncomfortable making the statement. He turns and begins to walk away.

"I'm alright partner. Just need some time to sort things out."

"Yeah. It's been a rough few months."

C H A P T E R   13

HEALING

Storm clouds begin moving into the area, so I elect to gather the fish and gradually move into the cavern. Even here in the Caribbean, a rainy day has its degree of fascination. At times the sun peeks through the clouds, creating beams of light that resemble flashlight beams. It's almost as if God is searching for someone. Lightning strikes against the dark clouds in the distance, creating an astonishing light show. The clouds glow and flash from the heat lightning almost resembling a fireworks display. I observe the storm for a while, making sure it remains at a distance.

I finally enter the uppermost cave entrance and work my way down through the passages to the main cavern. Attempting to distinguish the time of day inside the cavern is extremely difficult. It's most likely the reason I spend a lot of time outside. Life inside of a cave isn't the lifestyle I crave.

The first two people I run into are Kurt and Adrian. They are embraced in a romantic kiss, so I attempt to sneak by without interrupting their moment. Adrian is the first to spot me out of the corner of her eye.

"Just the person I need to talk to. Give those fish to Kurt and come with me. We need to have a good talk," Adrian exclaims breaking away her caress.

Kurt grumbles a bit as he holds out his hand for the fish. He laughingly remarks, "This isn't fair amigo! I just get a load of fish, and you end up with my wife. Somehow I'm getting genuinely burned in this deal."

"You just clean the fish first and later we'll talk about continuing that kiss. If you're good, maybe you'll even get lucky," Adrian snickers back to Kurt.

"Sorry partner," I interject with a grin, "I was really just trying to sneak by without interrupting the two of you."

"Well, you're really going to owe me big time for this one. Why did you have to catch so many fish?" Kurt jokes sarcastically.

All I can do is shrug my shoulders as Adrian leads me away to a quieter section of the cavern. I know I'm about to receive some kind of lecture about my general mood. Adrian is unhappy knowing someone is feeling miserable. I realize her heart is in the right place, so I will indulge her.

We sit down in a side cave that Kurt, Adrian, and Liana are using for sleeping quarters. The chairs are made out of crates from the Sea Jewel.

"Tony, I know the pain that you are going through, and it hurts us all deeply to see you suffer this way," Adrian begins as she looks me in the eyes. "There's nothing any of us could have done to change the way this rescue ended."

"I don't think you know how I really feel. Catalina was the only woman that enabled me to know what love is. My time with her was more than just a fling or a quick romance. I was truly planning to spend the rest of my life with her. I'd give up everything to have her back."

Adrian widens her eyes and rubs a tear away, nodding her head up and down. She assures me, "I know the emptiness you are feeling. When my father was killed, all I wanted to do was die. He was the center of my life—with the exception of my mother. If it was not for her, I would have killed myself. It took a lot of time for me to accept his murder. I will never fully get over it but I do know the way you are feeling. I miss Catalina as well." Her sincerity and sympathy is genuine.

I continue searching for the proper words, "I just don't know how to put things back together. I'm doing my best to cope with it. I just blame myself for not doing more. One more day and we may have found her."

At that point Adrian wraps her arms around me with a sympathetic hug. She whispers, "You did everything possible, more than most people would have done. If it wasn't for you, my daughter, me, and a lot of other people would be dead today. Don't ever blame yourself. You are the one that made all of this work."

"I'll work through it. I just need to get these bad memories behind me."

"I know it's going to take time. Just remember all of us are here for you. Your pain is our pain. Catalina would want you to carry on," Adrian adds with a smile. Her eyes tearing as she speaks.

"My mind right now is reeling with guilt that our operation caused Cancun to be targeted. If I didn't start this campaign, Cancun may not have been picked!"

"That's nonsense! Cancun was picked just like any other area could have been picked. The lottery is insane, no matter what grid they target." With that remark, she wipes her eyes. "We have to make sure another lottery never happens. Catalina would want you to fight for that."

"No. Another Cancun will never occur. Not as long as I'm alive." Kurt found himself a great lady when he found Adrian. "We better get back before Kurt thinks we're having an affair."

She laughs giving me a side glance, "Don't think that; he knows me too well. But you're right, let's get back before I get tempted." That brings a smile to my face.

Adrian and I follow the path back into the cavern and settle back into the rhythm of the day. Most everyone has their projects to accomplish. Our total mission revolves around making as many contacts worldwide as possible. In order to plan our next operation, many people will have to get organized. Contacts we make worldwide will succeed if we keep people communicating. Cooperation will be the key to our success.

Jim Turner stands watch outside the cave entrance as the sun begins to set. The darker it gets outside, the harder it is to notice approaching vessels. When the weather is stormy, it makes the watch almost impossible. Tonight the storms seem to stay in the distance, with a full moon to compliment the view. From our observation area, we can see for miles and miles out into the Caribbean Sea. The stars seem to tumble into your lap, glittering brightly in the night sky.

It's my turn to take watch, so I climb up through the passageway to the surface. I make my way over to the lookout area, being careful not to trip in the darkness. Jim is starring off into the distance, straining his eyes.

"Looks like it's going to be a nice night out. Any sign of life out there?" I inquire, taking care not to trip.

Jim snaps his head around in a startled manner. "I didn't hear you coming. As a matter of fact, I've been watching a small light off in the distance to the northwest. It may be just a fishing trawler, but you may want to keep an eye on it. Otherwise, everything's clear."

"Can you tell what direction it's heading?"

"No. It only appeared about fifteen minutes ago. Like I said, it's probably a fishing boat of some kind just trying out our waters."

"I'll keep an eye out," I proclaim resting myself against a rock. "There's food waiting for you. Adrian, Liana, and Juanita made a great fish stew."

"My stomachs been growling for the last thirty minutes. Anything sounds good." Jim snickers as he makes his way towards the cave entrance.

I look in the direction Jim suggests. A steady cool breeze blows in from the west as I stare off into the distance. I can make out a light from a small craft as it glows in the early darkness. The light flickers as the boat bounces across the waves. Staying alert to it for a good fifteen minutes, I notice the craft progressing closer to the island. I hesitate to set off the alarm until I'm positive it's coming to our shoreline. One craft will not create a catastrophe.

Another ten minutes clicks by as I watch the boat continue to head straight for our shoreline. The light on board the dinghy gets brighter and brighter as the craft makes its way towards the lagoon. I set the alarm off to alert everyone below we are about to have visitors. Within minutes Kurt and Carlos appear from the cave with a pair of night vision binoculars. They make their way over to me adjusting their eyes in the darkness.

"What's going on? Are we being invaded?" Kurt remarks trying to focus the binoculars.

"Look over to the northwest. There's a boat heading directly towards the lagoon," I answer quickly pointing in the direction.

Both of them gaze at the approaching boat with a feeling of uneasiness. The boat continues to stay on its course. It closes the distance on the lagoon. We begin to hear the hum of the motor.

"Hand me those binoculars, Kurt. I need to get a look at who's on board," I request holding out my hand. He tosses them over to me.

I place the binoculars to my face focusing on the occupants. I observe them for a moment studying the interior of the boat.

"It's a small cuddy cabin with at least three people on board. They look like civilians. I don't see anyone with a uniform of any type," I finally inform them. "One of the people on board is pointing towards the lagoon!" I pass the binoculars over to Kurt. "Keep watching, I'm going to sneak down into the lagoon and try to see what they're up to." I begin to climb down along the path.

Malik appears from the cave with a couple of dart guns in his hands. I hesitate a second to let him catch up.

"Tony. Me go wit yah, mon!" Malik exclaims handing me a gun.

The two of us silently make our way down along the pathway, being careful not to trip in the darkness. We creep along the tree line maneuvering towards the lagoon. The roar of the boat motor can be heard as we crouch down behind some underbrush. The boat appears at the mouth of the sound, making its way towards us.

I motion to Malik. "Load up the darts. Prepare for a confrontation." We observe the boat steer towards the beach. The outboard kicks up as it hits the sandy bottom.

"Three people are standing on the deck," I whisper to Malik. The driver cuts back on the engine speed as the boat drifts up onto the beach.

"Don't fire a dart till I give you a signal. I want to get a good look at them first."

"Me wait til yah be ready," Malik answers in a low tone.

"If I give you a signal, shoot the last two that get off the boat. I'll get the first one."

Both of us strain our eyes in the darkness, trying to discover who these people are. Suddenly, I get a glimpse of the first person climbing out of the boat. My heart begins to beat faster. It can't be!

Catalina's father, Diago Delray, swings around looking into the jungle for any signs of life. He holds onto the motorboats anchor line, attempting to dig it into the sand. I run up to him expecting to see Catalina in the craft.

I burst out of the underbrush. "Diago! You're not dead! How did you find us?" He stomps his foot on the anchor, driving it into the sand. Holding out his hand as I approach, he exclaims, "Catalina told us where to find you. Her directions were perfect."

"You mean she's alive! Where is she? My heart races with anticipation. I grab his hand with both of mine. "Please tell me she's safe!"

"I'm sorry to say, she's a political prisoner in Iceland. She was taken there by the military."

"Oh God! She's alive!" I mutter feeling tears form in my eyes. "What happened?"

"It's a long story. Help me get Maria out of the boat."

"Of course. I'm so glad to see both of you!" I motion for Malik as I run around to the back end of the boat. "Maria! You have no idea how great it is to see the two of you." I extend my hand, steadying the boat for her.

"Tony. You are a sight!" She grabs my hand, carefully stepping down into the water. "We need your help."

"How did you get out of Cancun? I looked everywhere for all of you!" I blurt out in confusion.

"Is there a place we can sit down? This last week has been a nightmare," She asks delicately. keeping her feet steady as the waves ripple around them. "You must meet Alonzo Cruz. He's responsible for getting us out of Cancun in time."

A stocky gentlemen with dark hair and a dark handlebar moustache stands at the back of the boat with his hand extended. "Alonso, I owe you more than I can ever repay. You are indeed a saint," I announce excitedly as I grasp his hand. "I'm so glad all of you are here and safe. Come inside the cavern and make yourselves at home. Everyone is going to celebrate tonight!"

"Senor, the pleasure is all mine. From the reports I hear, you and your banditos are, how do you say, the saints. People around the world know what all of you have done."

Alonzo hops off the boat, taking large strides to reach the sand.

Malik runs up with a look of total shock on his face. "They be ghosts mon!"

"Malik, you remember Diago and Maria Delray. We searched a few nights for them." Malik's puzzled look turns to a large smile. "Also meet Alonzo Cruz."

"You betcha mon!' We be glad you not dead." He shakes their hands as we stroll up towards the cave entrance. We carefully wind our way up to the entrance of the cave.

"We have a lot to talk about, partner. I've been mourning your deaths ever since we escaped from Cancun. Catalina must be horrified. Why would they take her?"

"It's a long story, amigo. Let me sit down with a drink, and I will tell it."

At the top of the trail stand Kyle, Kurt, Adrian, Liana, Carlos, Juanita, and a few others gathering to find out who our visitors are. The looks on their faces as we approach is worth a million dollars.

Kurt yells out excitedly, "My God, someone has figured out a way to bring back the dead!"

"Not quite the dead, but almost senor," Diago suggests with relief.

Everyone begins to introduce one another to Catalina's parents and Alonso Cruz. This is a moment I will never forget. Everyone makes their way down into the cavern. Once inside, Kurt and Carlos bring out the few bottles of rum that remain.

"You've got to tell me why Catalina is held by the military," I plead, handing a fresh drink to Diago.

He grabs the drink and hammers in down like it holds water from the fountain of youth. He wipes his forehead, letting out a sigh of relief. "Catalina is held hostage because she attempted to get information to all of you regarding this lottery. The reason Cancun was targeted along with the Yucatan Peninsula was to assassinate me and my whole family. I found this out hours before the military landed in Cancun. We escaped by plane without Catalina. The last we saw of her was in my car, desperately trying to get to the Casa de la Parrot. She had time to get there and get all of you out, but never made it. We found out later she was taken to the U.N. presidential outpost in Iceland. As long as they have her, I'm at their mercy. You need to help me free my daughter!"

"I don't understand. Why would they want to kill you?" I stare at Diago in complete amazement. Everyone listens in complete disbelief.

"Let me back up. I vigorously opposed the way the U.N. conducted its business when I was one of Spain's top Generals. I left, only to keep Spain safe from the wrath of the United Nations. Since I left, I have remained a secret general of an underground fighting the present U.N. leadership. Cancun was targeted on purpose to make sure I died and was no longer a threat to them. They have attempted to assassinate me many times. The United Nations is more corrupt than all of you can imagine."

My mind whirls with all this new information. "The United Nations had to know that our group on Cancun was secretly scheming against this lottery. Especially after we stole the U.S.S. Constellation. We always believed a spy has been among us although we never found any evidence. We thought they picked the Yucatan Peninsula to kill all of us."

Diago shook his head back and forth handing the glass over for another drink. "You don't have a spy in your group. They would be on you like flies by now."

I slam down my own drink, completely baffled by all of this. "All this time we have been thinking we were the reason Cancun was targeted. How did you find out that Cancun was the lottery's target before the military arrived there?"

"Thanks to Alonzo, we were saved in time. He served with me in Spain as my advisor. We also have inside government contacts. These contacts leaked information to him that the lottery was to be held in Cancun before they sealed up the peninsula. They marked me as the target." He hesitates a moment to let us grasp this new information. I listen with great intensity. "I have been opposed to the men who run this government for quite a while. We have become very organized attempting to change the U.N.. You and all your men have done more in the last few months to fight them than anyone on the planet. What I have heard on the news about your rescue and the people you saved, makes all of you the real heros."

"With you, hombre, we now may have a fighting chance!" Carlos hollers from the back area.

"With my contacts and the impressive operation all of you have accomplished, we are about to change history. The present leaders of this government, including Jordan Stanovich, are about to see a revolution that will be talked about for centuries." Diago announces as Maria joins him at his side.

"I know that I can speak for everyone on this island. We will be honored to join with you and stop this lottery. We have already made countless contacts around the world that are organizing as we speak. This island you have come to, along with the submarine, is protected by the most state-of-the-art stealth technology. As long as we remain here, they will not find us," I assure him looking around the room to check everyone's approval.

Kyle clears his throat to get everyone's attention, "I have to propose a condition to this organization. I will only remain involved as long as I understand we only oppose the key leaders and not the main government. If this government folds, the fragile economic structure will collapse. We will be assured a very bleak future for all of us."

"You have my word as a general, we only wish to clean out this government. The structure may wobble if we are successful, but it will remain intact. My priorities are only to clean out the scum."

We all shake hands to seal our joint venture. I turn to Alonso and grasp his hand in alliance. "Let us show you what we have accomplished."

Kyle takes Diago and Alonso inside of the submarine. They are impressed with the entire operation we have constructed here at Starpoint. Our network just grew by mammoth proportions. If we are going to fight this government, we need the support of as many people as possible.

Catalina has to be rescued by any means possible. Every conscious thought I have is centered towards her safe return. My enthusiasm is exploding in my mind, just knowing she's alive. My mind whirls with thoughts relating to a rescue plan.

Kurt, Adrian, and Liana make a bee line to me in a massive group hug. Within minutes everyone is piled together, thankful that Catalina is still alive. The camaraderie of this group is intense.

Updates in the news are constantly being monitored. The U.N. government is showing signs of losing control and stability. More of the military police are defecting from their posts. Military leaders begin speaking out publicly against the lottery, calling it the most inhumane occurrence in a thousand years. Politicians around the world begin to express their disfavor. Rioting continues across the globe. Government buildings are being burned and looted. Still pictures from our video are being hung on buildings and structures.

Everyone at Starpoint keeps the networks informed. We are preparing for an all-out assault on the U.N.—if it becomes necessary. The United Nations will fight back and retaliate against any opposition. We are definitely not out of harm's way. The fight against this lottery is just beginning. Most importantly, Catalina will be rescued.

C H A P T E R   14

ICELAND

The General Assembly of the United Nations at its origin proclaimed a Universal Declaration of Human Rights that protected everyone. These rights were abandoned when the U.N. took over as the world government.

The location of the main branch of government of the United Nations is the city of Reykjavik in the country of Iceland. New York City has remained the city with the general offices, but the main presidential and general assembly departments moved in the year 2032 to Iceland. The area was picked as the central headquarters of government forty years prior, due to to the fact that its location is central to the eastern and western continents. It also remains an area of great security. The landscape of Iceland is nothing like its name implies. The terrain is mostly plateaus interspersed with mountain peaks. Its coastline is deeply indented with bays.

The acting president of the U.N. is Jarmine Meranse. He has been considered as more of a stooge than a president. It is obvious to most people that vice presidents and committee members have controlled the laws and declarations of the government for a long time now. Men like Jordan Stanovich have rendered the presidential office almost useless with their powers of overriding and controlling votes. Any member opposing Stanovich's directives has a hard time remaining in Iceland. His power within the government remains hidden in the structure of governmental bureaucracy. Our next directive will be a direct attack on Stanovich and everyone who stands with him.

All of us pile into the main section of the submarine to discuss the next mission. It's time to link all these networks to help us attack the main government at its central core. We have contacts on all continents and of all faiths and religions working together to help us change this government.

Everyone in the sub is reeling from the anticipation of this next mission. It's obvious, the time for us to make a move has finally arrived. Kurt, Carlos, Diago, Alonzo, and I prepare to discuss this subject with everyone. We finalize our plans and prepare to get the main meeting underway. The room gets quiet as we get ready to make the information available.

Diago begins the meeting. "All of you have made great sacrifices over the last seven months for the freedom and dignity of mankind. You have my deepest respect and admiration for all you have accomplished. Our next mission will not be an easy one as we go up against this main branch of government. We will be aided by people from all parts of the globe to accomplish our goals in removing these men from power. Men who choose to use terrorism against their own people. In five days we will leave Starpoint and join a fleet of ships and vessels from both the eastern and western continents. The main target will be the main location of government at Reykjavik, Iceland."

Kyle stands up, injecting his principles, "How are we going to attack this government fortress in Iceland without weapons?"

Diago looks over at Kyle, "We will join up with a large group of ships in Spain. They will have all the weapons and supplies necessary for this mission."

Kyle thinks for a second, then asks another question, "This sounds like a suicide mission. How are we going to make a run on an island that has been set up like a fortress and is said to be sealed like a tomb?"

Diago answers without hesitation, "A fortress can be attacked in many different ways. A direct attack may not accomplish what we want, but an attack from within as we attack from the sea can accomplish much more. My intent is to synchronize our attack with a military coup within the government itself. I have planted people within this building that will aid us when the time is right. I will not disclose to anyone who they are for their own safety. Just be aware we will be aided from within when the time is right. My daughters safe return is absolutely necessary."

Kyle answers as he strokes his beard, "I hope you're right. This one scares the hell out of me."

He continues, "We should have a force of ships traveling with us that will set this government on its tail. People from many countries have promised their support."

I stand up to make the discussion clear. "Diago, pardon me. I need to speak for a moment. I need to clue all of you in on the specifics of this mission. Catalina risked her life in an attempt to tell us about this lottery. We owe her! Getting her out is the first priority. Stopping President Meranse and Jordan Stanovich with his followers is second. These men need to stand trial for their crimes. This government must stand down and cancel all future lotteries." I take a drink of water to wet my mouth before continuing. "Anyone unsure about this situation needs to back out now. Partners, we won't stop until we have accomplished it all. Jim, I'm going to need you and your explosives on this one."

"Got you covered mate." Jim answers in anticipation.

Kurt, speaking intensely but attempting to keep his cool, adds, "This fight is to reclaim the government from the tyranny of the men who call themselves leaders, but are no more than ruthless dictators. We have reached a point in this conflict of no return. The U.N. has military superiority over us, but the question is; will they commit to a battle when a majority of the population is against them? The feedback we've been receiving tells us the main core of government is coming apart and on the verge of a collapse."

I jump into the conversation before Kurt blows a fuse. "All we can do is pray that a peaceful solution will deliver itself when the time is right. Steve's stealth technology will play a significant role in reaching the small continent of Iceland. We plan to sneak in under their security and make our way to the president himself. This advanced technology may be the difference between a raging battle and a peaceful end. We do not leave until Catalina is safe. Alonzo, is there anything you need to add?"

"It's important we keep in contact with every ship in this armada, senor. A trigger-happy individual can easily spark a conflict. Keeping everyone in control may be a real problem," Alonzo remarks with genuine conviction.

"We'll keep every vessel aware of the need to refrain from the use of force. Within the next several weeks, the success or failure of our operation will be a part of history. With most of the population on our side, I believe we can stop the government and this lottery. I don't want any bloodshed, but the possibility of this rescue becoming a bloodbath is real. The military and especially the Navy are extremely well-armed and developed. They will not hesitate to fight if the orders are given."

The meeting continues for another hour as questions are discussed at great length. Allied countries such as Mexico, Spain, the United States, Ireland, Sweden, Finland, Canada, France, South America, Great Britain, Turkey, Russia, Germany, and even countries in the Middle East are sending men and ships to aid us in our run on Iceland. With such a show of force, the United Nations may not initiate a battle. Our plan is to surround the waters around Iceland from the northern Atlantic Ocean to the Norwegian Sea.

Preparations for our voyage are more mental than physical. The submarine is already ready to submerge with everything stocked. All the weapons, skip boats, and underwater scooters will be ready for us in Spain. Everything we need has been arranged by Diago Delray. We have come a long way from those first meetings at the Casa' de la Parrot bar in Cancun. Our operation has grown larger than I could have imagined. Now, the whole world is involved in these operations. I have nothing to regret except Catalina's abduction.

Ships of all types are being prepared in ports and bays all over the globe. Vessels as far away as Russia and Australia are already en route to secret locations known only by our network. Everyone aboard these ships has been informed not to engage unless a battle is absolutely necessary. Our biggest fear is that one ship will create a catastrophe.

On the fifth day, messages are sent to ships informing them of their instructions. The submarine is ready to take the drastic plunge. Last minute supplies are brought on board for our final mission. Everyone gathers at the loading area of the submarine for their final decree. It's a tense moment for everyone as we slowly walk towards the gang plank.

"Since all of us are together, it may be the proper time to say a small prayer." I hesitate to allow everyone to become silent. "May God help us fight our enemies who have inflicted such cruelty on our nation. Give us the power and the instinct to rid this government of these men. Help us develop a way to feed the masses without subjecting them to a horrible lottery. In God's name, Amen."

An assemblage of the crew reply loudly, "Amen!"

We continue to walk onto the deck, then climb down into the Constellation. I take one last look at the cavern before sinking below the iron hatch. Carlos, being the last one through, clamps the hatch shut, spinning the seal to lock it.

"Well, this is it. Our destiny is in our hands," I mutter to Kurt as we walk towards the control room.

"Lets just get Catalina out of there and do a little ass kicking on the way through." Kurt boasts with a little smirk on his face.

Kyle is already in the main control room, checking gauges and preparing to dive. He and his crew are totally prepared for the mission ahead. Steve has checked and rechecked the stealth system, making some improvements along the way. Last minute checks are performed to make sure that everything is in perfect working order.

"Flood down. All astern," Kyle hollers out his orders.

The sub lurches and shakes slightly as we disappear from view within the cavern. The water washes over the deck and engulfs the sub as we descend.

Kurt hollers out his next order as he fine-tunes the sub's maneuvers, directing the sub out through the cavern entrance, "Ten degrees down bubble. All ahead two-thirds. Give me a heading of zero-four-five degrees and maintain." The helmsman brings her around to the new bearing.

The sub runs along the coral reefs as we head out towards deeper water.

"The day is just beginning, and we have a long ways to go. Spain will be the only stop on our journey to Iceland." Kurt reflects looking around at the gauges. "We may as well inform everyone about our exact plans."

Kyle announces over the speaker system, "Everyone to the storage area. Drop what you're doing."

People manage to get through the passageways as they enter the room. Most everyone on board takes seats around the room with the exception of Kyle's crew, who remain in control.

"All of us have worked our asses off to accomplish this network. People around the world have come together like no other time in history to crush this lottery and the people that are responsible for it." Kurt begins the meeting. "We have vessels and ships from almost every country heading towards Iceland as a

demonstration to the United Nations that the people want to stop this lottery now! If it's a military confrontation they want, then we will be ready to respond."

The people in the room begin to talk among themselves. It becomes obvious something is not acceptable.

Malik speaks up. "Why it necessary to use weapons other dan darts? We have dat reputation."

Carlos interjects. "This isn't going to be the same kind of battle, amigo. They will have many elaborate weapons at their disposal. We won't be able to fight without proper ammo."

"No matter what we have mon, they blow us out of de water," Malik remarks with some irritation.

"Good point, Malik. Let's put it to a vote. All in favor of using our dart guns only raise your hands," I instruct gazing around the room.

People glance around at each other as hands slowly extend. They kept going up until a vast majority of people around the room have a hand extended.

"It will be a suicide run if we don't have weapons to fight them!" Diago demands after seeing the hand count.

"These darts are incredible. I have found out first hand. The drug in these darts take effect in a split second. There's absolutely no time to react," I inform Diago as the occupants of the room begin to cackle.

"Most, if not all the other ships in this armada will be carrying weapons. I can't stop them from doing so," Diago replies sitting back in an uncomfortable fashion.

"Well, let's hope we can sway this government to cancel any further lotteries without a confrontation. We can use evasive tactics like flares to cloud our way if it becomes necessary. Hopefully, the other ships will follow our orders," Kurt assures him, attempting to drive home the point.

"Steve's flares work extremely well. They stopped that gun boat in its tracks like a blinding light from God. If we can get to the U.N. headquarters before any other vessel, maybe this whole nightmare will end." I hesitate. "We don't need or want a world war. All we need to do is locate Catalina and take down Meranse, Stanovich and any other followers. Our sub may be the only vessel with the ability to make it through Iceland's defenses. It will be totally up to us to make the final stand."

"Amen to that!" Carlos bellows.

"Well my friends, I hope it will be that easy. Personally, I think were in the battle of our lives. Along with the men I have inside, we may just have a chance. I salute you all for your courage!" Diago raises his cup to engage a toast.

The balance of the meeting is spent discussing strategies and going over what-if scenarios. It seems to be the first time in history that the world pools together for a common goal. The passage of time will be the only test as to how cooperation will continue around the globe after this conflict is over.

Kyle and his crew keep us on a fairly direct course in the northern Atlantic Ocean. This sea route will lead us from the Caribbean Islands across the North Atlantic to the waters off Portugal. To our north lay the Azores Islands as Kyle maneuvers us in a northerly path along Portugal's coast. Reports of activity in the waters around us are relayed by radio. Vessels are heading towards our location in record numbers. Government military ships are being dispatched to strategic locations as the armada travels towards Iceland.

We continue along to the northernmost section of Spain into an inlet named R. de Vigos. It's located just north of Portugal on the north peninsula of Spain. Kurt carefully commands the U.S.S. Constellation into the inlet to the port city of Vigo, Spain. Our visit here will be temporary before we venture towards Iceland. Diago has arranged for skip boats, sea scooters, and supplies to be waiting upon our arrival.

Kyle orders the submarine to surface in the inlet, "Blow ballast tanks until the sub is awash." The orders are repeated. The submarine rises within the inlet. We begin hearing the sound of water flowing across the decks.

"Stop engines," Kyle decrees watching the gauges from his vantage point.

"All stop captain."

Kurt spins the bridge hatch wheel and springs it open with a clank. One at a time, we begin to emerge onto the deck. I take in a huge breath of the fresh sea air. Along the docks are many ships waiting for our orders. With the sub on the surface, Kyle maneuvers it towards a docking area they have prepared for us. We have arrived at our first destination, and the sight is a marvel to behold. Along the wharf are a multitude of people clapping and cheering as we stand there dumbfounded. We did not expect any notoriety on such a modest arrival. Our exploits, especially in Mexico, have made us something of cult heroes. It's an impressive sight to behold as the sub pulls alongside the pier. Our time here has to be short. Our arrival is known by too many people to allow us a safe haven from the government.

Diago promises, "The people here are trustworthy. I can personally assure our safety."

Kyle looks up at him as he climbs towards the open hatch. "I hope you're right Diago. Right now, we're sitting ducks."

Diago climbs out onto the deck as the crowd begins to chant, "Diago! Diago!" He keeps his composure and waves back to his people. I can understand their respect for this man who has been run out of Spain for his viewpoints. For his dedication, he almost ended up a dead ex-general.

A few men lower a plank allowing us to leave the sub. Alonzo stays at Diago's side as we parade along the pier, greeting people along the way. A welcoming committee waits at the end to receive us. They appear to be his attache of followers.

"Welcome! Welcome my friends! Has everything been prepared?" Diago questions them as we approach.

"Si, General Delray. Everything is ready as you ordered."

"Good! Good! Get everything on the sub. Latch the scooters to be released quickly."

"Si General Delray!"

People here in Spain are as gracious and helpful as one could expect. They begin outfitting the sub in record time with everything requested. Several beautiful ladies bring baskets of flowers in memory of the people who died in Mexico. Weapons are offered to us but in light of our previous discussions, we turn them down. Already, too many deaths have been attributed to this lottery.

Many ships have gathered from different countries waiting for orders from us as to how and when to proceed. It's time to make our final stand. Approaching the waters around Iceland will be intense. Military gun ships and battleships will be waiting, ready to use maximum fire power. We know what we are up against. We spread the word to all available vessels; Start the assault on Iceland. Messages are passed along from ship to ship. We emphasize the orders; Travel as close to the continent of Iceland as possible without triggering a conflict. It should be possible to stay within a certain distance and not be fired upon. This may give us a chance to make an underwater run for the continent as the military is distracted by the massive number of ships on their coastline.

Without any hesitation, Kyle has us gliding out of the inlet into the North Atlantic Ocean. The scooters have been installed on the deck of the sub with precision. New scuba gear has been brought aboard, making our plans complete. The final assault to regain the world's freedom and survival has begun. Catalina will soon be rescued.

C H A P T E R 15

BATTLE ON ICELAND

While leaving Spain, Kyle orders, "Keep us above the surface. I'll let you know when to dive."

"Aye, captain."

We head out into the Atlantic Ocean keeping the course set on Iceland. Several of us remain on the deck to witness the number of ships preparing to follow. It's an awesome sight to see as vessels from all countries converge in and around the Spanish port to proceed with us. Several ships begin to blow air horns to celebrate the union we have established. It catches on and soon ship horns and whistles can be heard echoing all over the area in a show of might demonstrating the rivalry of our mission. Ships are displaying flags of all nations as the convoy begins to move. It's a sight I will never easily forget.

As we move out into the northern Atlantic Ocean, the time arrives to submerge and disappear off radar. Everyone on deck crawls back through the hatch, sealing it behind us. The submarine picks up speed as we clear the mouth of the inlet.

"Pull the plug. Flood down. Keep us on a heading of two-seven-five degrees. All ahead two-thirds." Kyle orders sitting and back waiting for his commands to be carried out.

"Two-seven-five degrees. All ahead two thirds," the order is repeated.

The sub heads down into the depths of the deep blue, leaving the ships in the convoy.

The networks are busy with activity as ships communicate information and news. Three individuals on our sub monitor the radios just to stay alert to any problems. If a situation does occur, we will have to solve it quickly. The convoy's purpose is just to create a show of force towards the United Nations and its military. Our mission is to stop the lottery, not to start a war.

Our method of communicating requires us to radio key ships in the armada. They, in turn, will pass the information on to all ships and vessels in the convoy. At this point in time, it doesn't matter whether the government hears our communications or not. They know we are approaching quickly and will not be stopped easily. As we maneuver ahead of the ships, it's important our position is not disclosed. Our strategy is to get to the island while the ships keep the military off our backs. We have to make it through to Iceland no matter how far the other ships travel.

Ships from Greenland, Finland, Sweden, Norway, and Russia are traveling from the north blocking the Norwegian Sea route. They plan to also bring pressure from the north onto Iceland.

Malik enters the main galley as we listen to the radio chatter. He appears anxious as he walks up and sits down next to me. The look on his face suggests something is troubling him.

"What's the problem, Malik? You look like you just lost your best friend," I inquire holding onto a cup of coffee.

"No mon, but there be a problem," Malik answers shaking his head back and forth.

"I hope there aren't any problems. We don't need any trouble now." I bark in a hyper tone.

"Follow me, mon. Me show yah wah me discover."

Malik gets up from his seat and starts down the main corridor. We follow through several hatches heading towards the main storage room. He stops in front of the main supply hatch as we gather behind him in the corridor. He places his hand on the hatch lever and hesitantly begins to open it.

"Now mon, don get uptight when yah see wah me hab to show yah!"

My anxiety is running at an all-time high as we stand there expecting the worst. Kurt, Carlos and the others stand behind me patiently waiting to witness what's behind the door. Several of them strain their necks in order to see what Malik has discovered. Malik enters as I reluctantly step into the room behind him. I immediately glance over to the right side of the room where a table has been placed. On the table sit three full bottles of rum with a variety of different cups and glasses. Just beyond the table is a carved-out rendition of a gravestone made out of cardboard and a few other materials. The gravestone has been painted the normal gray color with etchings around it, giving it an authentic appearance. On it is written in indented lettering 'UNITED NATIONS LOTTERY' with the dates September 25th, 2073-thru tomorrow's date of March 30th, 2074. Followed by the letters 'RIP'.

Malik stands with a smile on his face extremely proud of the masterpiece he has assembled. Relief spreads over me as I stare at the fake gravestone and rum. As the others file into the room, the laughter begins to escalate. Malik is at it again, but this time it helps to break the tension all of us are feeling.

"Malik, now that's a masterpiece," Kurt snickers as he heads for the table for a drink.

You know mon, it be the truth," Malik remarks taking in the laughter of everyone. "This makes a Jamaican curse on it."

"You had me worried there for a moment, partner," I reply as I walk over to the table. "Let's condemn this thing properly with a toast."

Malik pours the rum into the assorted glasses. The shots of rum are passed around the room until everyone has one.

"To Catalina's safe return and the demise of this lottery!" I holler out raising my drink in the air.

"To Catalina and the end of the lottery!" Everyone hollers.

"To Malik and his gravestone," A voice rings out from the crowd.

"All of you enjoy another round, while Kurt and I clue Kyle in on the problem."

Kurt grabs up a bottle and a few glasses from the table. We leave the supply room through the same corridor. Working our way through the sub, we finally arrive at the control room.

"What in the world is bothering Malik?" Kyle asks turning towards us as we enter.

"You really don't want to know, but I'll tell you anyways. Malik made up a tombstone of the lottery with tomorrow's date on it. It's actually pretty amusing," I answer chuckling at the thought of it.

"We brought you and your team a shot of rum to toast our success. Malik had it all set up," Kurt adds, sitting the rum down on a table.

"Well, this I will drink to. Malik deserves a pat on the back," Kyle remarks with a smirk on his face.

Kurt passes around the glasses of rum for everyone in the control room. "Have a drink fellas. You guys deserve it."

"Sir. I'm picking up an increase in activity on the surface," the radio officer informs.

"What are you picking up?"

"Reports are being relayed to us, acknowledging U.N. Navy gun ships in the process of blocking ocean passages on our route. Ships in our convoy have already been stopped and threatened if they proceed."

"Return this message. Tell them to stop without conflict and wait for new orders."

"Aye Captain." The officer relays orders to the vessels.

"Let me know the minute you get confirmations." Kyle retorts to his radio officer.

"This could be a problem, Kyle. It's just the hassle we were worried about." I reflect waiting for the radio officers reply.

Kyle runs his hand through his hair in deep thought over his next order. A minute clicks by as we wait in anticipation.

"Sir, ships are following our orders. They are stopping rather than risk a conflict with the Navy. They will wait for new orders."

"Carry on. Tell them to hold their positions."

As we approach the small continent of Iceland, we can't afford a battle. For now, it's better just to show the government this large convoy of anti-sentiment. We want these ships to be more of a nuisance so we can slip by without detec- tion. Kyle maneuvers the submarine below a few Navy gun boats as we silently and skillfully head in towards the coastline.

"Sir! There's another report informing us of an Australian ship being fired on by a Navy gun ship. They tell us the shot was fired across their bow."

"It's a warning not to proceed. I hope the Australian schooner took heed to their warning?" Kyle asks in a concerned tone.

Yes sir. They did. They took it seriously and stopped."

"Sounds like the tension in the waters above us is getting more and more intense. For now, our plan is working," I confide in Kyle. "We are getting through unnoticed."

"Let's hope we make it."

Steve's stealth system is working perfectly as we glide underneath the Navy ships. The submarine streams along passing enormous navy vessels without even a notion of our presence. The Navy is being overwhelmed by this large armada of ships heading towards them from all directions. Diago, Kurt, Carlos, Alonzo, and I meet privately to discuss our tactics. We have to be on the same page when the moment comes to go ashore.

"Diago. Just how long will it take your spies to open the side doors and let us in?" Kurt asks with a bit of intensity to his voice.

"When they receive my signal, they should have the door to the west security entrance open in about fifteen minutes. This tunnel leads to the main vice presidential lobby area," Diago replies.

"It should take us at least twenty minutes to get to the shoreline after we leave the sub. I estimate another fifteen minutes to get to those entry doors. They have to be opened when we get there or we may be sitting ducks," I add, making sure our timing is correct.

"Then I will give the signal to my men the moment we reach the shoreline. The timing should be just right," Diago calculates. "We need to enter the building quickly and dismantle the situation inside. Stanovich and his followers should be rendered harmless within minutes of our entry. They'll be arrested and held on charges for the courts to handle. Catalina should be in a safe place when we take over."

"The problem is, will the courts even convict them?" I point out.

"My courts will!" Diago answers quickly with a wink.

"Let's get everyone into position. We only have about fifteen minutes left before we are at the launch point," Kyle informs us.

"There is one change I have to make in our approach to the mainland," Diago begins to inform us. "We cannot use the skip boats for our approach. They will pick us off in a second at the surface."

"What do you have in mind?" I inquire.

"I had sea scooters attached to the sub alongside the skip boats. One scooter to a person. They will pull everyone along almost as fast as the skip boats. I estimate it will take us another twenty minutes at the most to reach the shoreline. All of us will stay below the surface until we reach a point we can exit without a problem," Diago answers.

"Sea scooters it is, amigo. I hope these new dry suits are warm as you say," Carlos says, handling the suit as he attempts to put it on.

"They should be; they're tested by Navy divers," Kurt replies with a smirk on his face.

"Let's suit up and get this operation underway. Kyle will keep us posted by radio if any problems arise. Let's get Catalina the hell out of there!" I exclaim.

"You got it, hombre!" Carlos barks back.

Twenty of us suit up, including Carlos, Kurt, Malik, Alonzo, Diago, and I. We prepare to dive into the chilly waters off of the coast of Iceland. The dart guns along with containers of darts are distributed to everyone. All the equipment has been checked and rechecked to a fault. We can't afford mishaps or problems at this stage of our operation.

Kyle announces our readiness to leave the sub, "We're in the sector. I can't risk a closer position. Make us proud!"

One at a time, we lower ourselves down through the lower hatch into the icy ocean of the Denmark Strait. At first the cold engulfs me like jumping into a frozen pond, but as the heat of the thermal dry suit kicks in, the cold becomes less noticeable. I wait at the hatch exit for all the divers to clear the sub signaling them to swim towards the sea scooters.

We swim around to the deck of the sub and begin detaching the scooters. Each one disconnects from its resting place, ready to be energized to pull us through the frigid water. Diago has acquired the latest series of scooters manufactured and streamlined for maximum speed underwater. A contour shield acts as a deterrent to fight the force of water over the scooter. The diver comfortably steers the craft, encompassed in nonmoving water. The ocean around us shimmers clear with a blue-green tone to it. It differs from the tropical waters in the Caribbean.

With all the scooters running, we form a triangular pattern. The purr of the electric motors begins to pull us along through the Icelandic waters heading off towards the coastline. We begin to notice volcanic boulders forming the ocean bottom interlaced with coral crustaceans. Small to medium sized fish dart along the bottom finding cracks and crevices to wedge themselves into. Sea plants wave back and forth as the current flows in altered directions. I glance to my right, catching sight of the antics of a seal darting around the ocean bottom. He maintains a twenty-yard distance, keeping a curious eye on us as we pass.

A quick glance at my compass assures us of our direction. Ahead of us, we notice the large metallic bottom of a Navy ship anchored in place. As we glide past, the anchor chains project down to the ocean bottom. Continuing on, the sea floor gradually becomes shallower as we close in on the bay. We follow the bottom at a depth of seventy five feet for several minutes studying the inner bay. Ahead of us appears an inlet with boulder formations allowing for a possible exit to land. Underwater rock formations produce a jagged inner bay with crevices allowing for a transition zone to land. The protrusions of rock above water could mask our departure from the sea.

We throttle back our scooters to a stop as we study the exit point from underwater. I look over at Kurt and Carlos as they hold up their thumbs to signify a survey above water. I point to the surface and then to myself to indicate a visual inspection. Kurt returns an affirmative signal as he waves to the others to hold their positions. I cut power to the scooter and gradually make an ascent. My ears crackle as they begin to equalize from the pressure. Carefully, I break the surface keeping a vigilant eye on my surroundings. As I turn, I notice Military ships in the distance in combat readiness. Ahead of me in an inner bay, crevices of rock display camouflage for us to make an effective retreat from the ocean. I follow the rock up with my eyes noticing a natural wall of stone for us to easily make an escape. Having made a satisfactory inspection, I sink down making my way back to the awaiting posse. Clouds of rumbling bubbles appear as I close in on their position. They watch as I descend upon them accelerating with my flippers to quicken the pace. I glide in beside Kurt pointing in the direction of our escape route. Kurt nods affirmatively as we begin to stow the scooters among the boulders on the ocean floor. We attach them together, securing each one.

Silently swimming upward, the group follows me toward the rock crevices to reach the exit point. A quick thrust of my flippers, and I break above the surface onto a slab of rock. Kurt, Malik, and Carlos appear, keeping a low profile in the water. I quickly gaze around making sure our departure is safe. Everything appears secure as I reach out for Kurt's hand. He grabs on as I pull him from the icy water. The air is ripe with the scent of land. The low angle of the sun cast shadows against the rocks aiding in our camouflage.

"Crawl up against those rocks. I'll help the others," I whisper keeping my voice as low as possible. "Look for a good path out of here."

Kurt establishes his footing after pulling off his flippers. "There's a good spot over there to stow the tanks."

In turn, I help out each member out of the sea as waves ripple in on us, crashing against the rocks. Malik remains in the water as he hands me the sealed bags of equipment and weapons. I latch onto each relaying them to anyone willing to take one. Malik finally grabs my hand, finding his footing in order to exit the water.

"Mask it up, mon." He pulls his flippers off, tossing them onto a rock. "Lawd Gad! We be on de way now!"

"Don't get too carried away just yet. We got a long way to go," I remind Malik as I climb up behind the ledge. "Diago, contact your men inside. Give us twenty-five minutes to rendevous."

"I'm making contact right now." He answers pulling the communicator from a sealed packet.

Everyone removes their diving gear, revealing camouflaged outfits underneath. The weapons are unsealed and passed around for each to engage. Steve hands out the flare guns to a few people who he chooses to have one.

"I hope we make the building in time, amigo." Carlos stammers to Diago as he adjusts his weapons sights.

"They'll wait for us. This I promise." Diago responds

I crawl up to the top of the ledge and peer over to visualize our escape route. A plateau extends northward with several boat buildings close to our location. A mountainous ridge line extends off into the distance. The U.N. building stands out from the terrain like a skyscraper in the desert. A road extends towards the building with several military trucks parked along its route. Looking off to my left, I notice several military ships around the bay with men scattered on the decks.

"Is it a go?" Diago inquires as he establishes contact with his spy.

"There's a boat house just over the ridge. The immediate area is clear, so get ready to roll." I slip back down to gather up my own weapon. "Is everyone ready?"

"Yah!" resounds from everyone.

"Let's get it!"

Carlos engages his weapon. "Amigos, shoot for maximum effect. No more than twenty minutes to the UN." He passes back dart magazines to everyone. "Take what you need. We brought plenty."

I reaffirm with everyone, "Stay down and close to each other. Our entry will be on the west side of the compound."

"My people will give us cover as we get closer. Any questions?" Diago remarks.

Kurt turns his head towards Diago, "Let's just get this posse moving." He clicks a magazine containing twenty darts into his weapon.

Securing a foot hold on the ledge, I glance around, ensuring a clear path along the rocky landscape. A truck containing U.N. personnel can be seen moving away from our position on the main road. I climb up over the ridge sprinting towards the boat house. In pairs, the others follow dashing quickly to my position. We maintain a low profile as we move in silence.

Kurt catches up to me on my left flank. "Got your back, Tony. Looks like there may be trouble ahead."

Ahead of us lay the main road leading to the U.N. headquarters. A crossroad approximately three-hundred yards away renders several military vehicles including a military transport truck parked along the roadside. In the distance beyond these vehicles, troops can be seen moving about the area.

"Kurt, check out that transport vehicle along the crossroad. It just may be our ticket in."

Kurt pulls out a pair of field binoculars and surveys the area as we remain behind the corner of the boat house. He focuses his view on the truck. "No one's around it at the moment. If we can get to it without being seen, we just may have a ride in."

"Check the road beyond it for activity."

He looks along the road. "There's activity well beyond it, but nothing around it."

"Well partner. Keep me covered. I'm gonna check it out. Get everyone ready to move on my signal."

A few trees and a clump of brush stands between us and the truck. It's the only cover available as I prepare to make a sprint. I sling my gun over my shoulder keeping an eye on the area ahead. I push off from the building pounding the turf as fast as my legs can move while keeping a low profile. My heart begins to beat harder as I scramble closer to the refuge of the brush ahead. Even with my camouflage clothing, I'm an obvious target.

I dive into the bushes suspending my motion. I fight to control my heavy breathing as I gaze through the brush. To my astonishment, no one notices the activity. A troop transport vehicle remains within fifty yards of me. Glancing to the rear, Kurt's head protrudes slightly out from the corner of the building, watching my progress. Taking a second to catch my breath, I prepare for the final leap.

The wind picks up as I crawl close to the edge of the shrubs. A deep inspiration of air clears my head for the next run. I jump to my feet, rushing out of the bushes, finding the power to sprint to the vehicle. My feet pound the uneven terrain, swirling small pebbles in my wake. Springing to the foot board of the truck, I gaze inside the window to see if keys are left behind. The door handle flips up, opening the vehicle for entry. I search all the compartments, but the keys can't be found. The ignition system is security proof so even a quick bypass of the ignition is out of the question.

Squinting out the window, I notice Kurt and Diago making a sprint for the brush. Behind them three others are attempting to scramble, hot on their heels. I hurry around to the back, to get the rear door open. By a great stroke of luck, the door yields. The inside contains bench seating for troop transport, making it a temporary refuge from the surrounding military troops. From around the edge of the truck, Kurt and Diago sling themselves to the rear. The sprint leaves them huffing for air.

"Can we get it started?" Diago exclaims hurriedly attempting to control his heavy breathing.

"No keys, and the security ignition is almost tamper proof. Get everyone in the back. You and Kurt come up in the cab with me."

A few at a time, the men hustle up to the truck clambering into the back as Diago motions them to enter. "Everyone in the back!" They file in quickly as the last few arrive.

I grab Kurt by the arm. "Get in the cab, partner. We need to work on a plan."

Kurt, Diago, and I scramble into the front after everyone is situated. Looking out over the landscape, no guards seem alerted by our actions.

"No keys huh? Look everywhere?" Kurt exclaims ruffling through the glove box.

"Any place keys would be hidden! Got any ideas?"

"Well, there's too many guards to get by there on foot," Kurt responds.

Diago turns quickly adjusting the electric side mirror. "A vehicle is approaching! Look in the mirror!" He adjusts it for my view. "Think they've seen us?"

Kurt grabs his weapon engaging a dart in the chamber. "Don't know, Hombre. We're about to find out."

I glance around quickly trying to formulate a plan. "Duck down. When they get close to the truck, spring on them from both doors. Dart them quickly!"

We slide down into the seats listening as the truck pulls up and squeals to a stop. The doors of the arriving vehicle snap open while I quietly engage a dart. I lay my hand across the door handle as we listen to the outside conversation.

"You two take this truck back to the main entrance of the embassy. Here's the keys. A squad from the fourth will be waiting for you. Make it snappy!" A voice barks out commands.

Doors slam shut as the vehicle accelerates away from the transport truck. We stay silent as footsteps approach. "Flip me a cigarette will ya. There's no hurry. Those guys can wait," Another voice outside resounds.

The click of a lighter snaps as I glance over to Kurt and Diago. I whisper, "Just got our ride partners. Let the vehicle get some distance. When the doors begin to open, kick them hard. I'll dart them." We listen as they stumble around outside the truck.

"Needed that cigarette. Here, you drive," a voice says as footsteps clamber up to the side door. The handle rattles disengaging the latch. With all Kurt's force, He slams his foot against the door. It blasts open sending the individual flying to the ground. I jump forward taking aim triggering my weapon. A slight hiss is heard as the dart hits the guard in his abdomen.

"What's wrong Pete?!?" The other guard exclaims as he runs around the truck.

I lunge out of the driver's side with weapon in hand. Kurt flips out of the pas- senger door ready to engage. We each pop a dart in the remaining guard as he freezes with a wide-eyed look. He drops to his knees as the keys clamber to the ground.

"Damnnn!" He falls forward on his face.

"Just found the keys amigo!" Kurt scoffs as he reaches down to pick them up.

"We can drive right up to the damn door," Diago reflects with delight in his voice.

The two guards are shoved in the back of the truck as a brilliant idea comes to mind. "Tell them in the back to pull their uniforms off. Bring them up here along with any orders they may have on them."

Within minutes, Carlos appears at the passenger door with the uniforms and a set of orders found in a front pocket. "Here amigos! I keep the cigarettes."

Kurt and I expediently change into the uniforms, pulling them over our camouflaged outfits. I slip the key into the ignition, turning it to the right. The truck fires up with a rumble.

I nod to Diago with a smile. "Let's get your daughter back."

"Since there's only two uniforms, I'll have to ride in the back," Diago acknowledges, jumping out of the cab hurrying around to the rear.

Kurt slams the passenger door closed. "Let's go, amigos. The suns a wastin!"

Engaging the transmission, we accelerate toward the U.N., keeping our eyes on the activity ahead. The truck lurches forward, carrying us in disguise towards the uncertain. In the distance we see a main entry gate with guards stationed at their posts.

"Get ready, partner. If anything falls apart, we'll have to take these guys down in a hurry. They may want to search the back, so be primed for a rumble."

Kurt checks both of our weapons to make sure they are engaged and ready to fire. "Just let them try and stop us."

We pull up to the gate as a guard waves us to a stop. He walks up to the drivers side door and rotates his finger with a gesture to roll down the window. I oblige by toggling the electric switch engaging the window to roll down. "Afternoon. Got our orders right here. Need to pick up some troopers at the main entrance."

The guard takes the papers and reads over the information. I take a side glance at Kurt, who is studying every move the guard makes.

"Anyone in the back?" The solder asks, maintaining a smug look. He glances up, waiting for a reply.

"No. We haven't picked them up yet."

"Open up the back. I need to take a look."

"These troops have been waiting for a while now. I don't want to get anyone pissed off."

"It only takes a minute. I need to look in the back," he insists stepping back from the door.

"Yeah. I know. Regulations…right?" I flip open the door, realizing there's no way to stop a confrontation. I glance over to Kurt and whisper, "Get ready."

I bound out of the cab walking back to the rear of the truck with the guard following. "Think we're going to have any trouble at sea. They say there's a lot of ships heading our way." We stop at the back of the truck.

"Don't know. Let me have a quick look and you can be on your way."

I stand off to the side of the door as he reaches for the handle. He pulls the door open and begins to enter. Startled, he glares inside as a dart instantly hits him in the chest. He staggers back wide eyed and collapses to the ground.

"Toss me a gun, quick," I yell to the first person standing in the doorway. Carlos tosses me a weapon as I hurry around to the guard shack. I pass two other troopers lying on the ground already stunned by Kurt's trigger finger. One of them attempts to pull his revolver as I nail him again. He falls into a deep sleep from the added dose.

Another guard runs up from around the rear of the shack. "What the hell is going on?!?"

"This!" I snap my finger on the trigger releasing a dart into his shoulder. He stumbles, falling forward as the drug quickly engulfs him.

Kurt runs in from around the corner. "That's the last one. Let's get out of here pal, before the whole squads on us!"

Carlos, Diago, Malik, and a few others file into the room. "Help us drag all of them inside and out of sight." We pull the troopers from the outside into the shack. A closet serves as a great hideaway for them. Grabbing our weapons, everyone piles back into the truck. I crank up the truck with a snap of the key. Within seconds, the transport vehicle is bolting away from the gate. I edge the accelerator toward the floor as we rumble away from the gate.

Military personnel are stationed at intervals as we close in on the west end of the building. I look back into the rear-view mirror, noticing a few guards entering the guard shack behind us. "They may be onto us. I may have to ram this next gate!"

As we approach the next gate, several guards are scurrying to take positions. I accelerate steering the truck directly at the half open gate. The sentries raise their weapons as we barrel down on them.

"Duck down! I hope this glass is bullet proof!"

WHAP WHAP! Bullets begin to snap off the glass as we travel closer. Clenching the steering wheel, I aim for the weakest point of the gate. Ping! Snap! The bullets increase in number.

KA BASH! The gate explodes as we ram it, sending pieces flying thirty feet in the air. Two of the guards dive out of the way as we continue through the other side. The truck barrels on as I hold my foot on the accelerator.

"I'll bet that gets some attention!" Kurt shouts as he exhales an extended breath. "Turn left ahead. Diago's men should be waiting for us," he instructs as he defiantly stares ahead.

"We have to get inside quickly. We're hamburger meat out here!" I holler as the pinging bullets continue to ricochet off the truck. In the rearview mirror, I notice military personnel scrambling to pursue us. Flashes of gun fire coincide with loud snaps of bullets striking the truck. With my foot pressed firmly to the accelerator, I pull the steering wheel to the left skidding as the tires barely maintain traction. The U.N. main government building is off to our right. I accelerate to make it to the side entrance.

"There's two of Diago's men waiting at the corner!" Kurt bellows pointing them out.

Standing at the edge of the building are two men dressed in business attire holding automatic weapons. They begin to fire to at a vehicle in pursuit of us. I glance again into the rearview mirror as the vehicle skids off the road from the sudden barrage of lead. The vehicle slams into an embankment, smashing the front quarter panel.

"Pull in there! We'll have to make a run for it!" Kurt hollers pointing to a set of parking spaces near the open door.

"I'll do better than that! Get everyone in the back ready to make a quick exit!" Pulling into the parking area, I jam the truck into reverse. The vehicle lurches backwards as I steer it directly towards the door. Diago's men continue to fire upon vehicles attempting to enter the area. They slowly back up towards the door as I hop a curb to get as close to the door as possible.

"When I hit the brakes, Storm that door!"

The truck bounces from side to side as it continues toward the door. Looking in the side mirror, I slam on the brakes within five feet of the door. Kurt pounds on the back wall of the cab with his fist to signal everyone in the truck. "Get out now!"

A sporadic bullet ricochets off the truck as we exit the cab from both side doors. I scramble around to the back to make sure everyone is exiting. Quickly, we pile in through the east door of the U.N. as lead scatters around the exterior. Diago's men back up to the door, firing rounds at patrols in pursuit. One enters as the other lingers at the entrance, spraying the progressing guards with gun fire. As he turns to enter, a bullet strikes him in the neck. He staggers in as blood gushes from a cavity that used to be his neck. He collapses, gurgling from the blood entering his bronchial passages. Diago slams the door shut, latching it quickly with the available security locks. Bullets snapping off the door create small indents as the outside barrage continues. Diago's spy quickly suffocates as we attempt in vain to revive him. His body slumps into lifelessness as his gasps for air cease.

THE CONFRONTATION

Diago looks on as one of his comrades losses his fight for life. He pats his chest in a salute to his sacrifice.

"It's too late for him! We need to find Catalina and shut down this crap!" I turn to the individual Diago planted here. "Where are they holding her?"

"I'll show you. We've knocked out the inside video cameras. They won't be able to track us through the building."

"Is she alright?"

"She's been slapped around, but not badly. The last I saw her, she was locked in a room off a side hallway. I'll take you there."

"Make it fast, partner. They know we're in here!"

He turns to lead the group down the corridor. All of us hustle up the lengthy hallway.

"What is your name?" I inquire.

"Rico. They call me Rico."

"Well Rico, I'm sorry about your partner back there."

"We've been through a lot together. He was planted here at the same time I was."

"We'll avenge his death. I promise you that!"

As we make our way along the corridor, distant explosions begin to resonate echoing off the walls. The building shudders with each eruption.

Kurt turns to me with a look of surprise. "Sounds like artillery shells from a battleship. Somebody just got trigger happy. The battle at sea just erupted."

"Oh God. This situation is going to get bad." I glance around at everyone. "Let's pick up the pace. A lot of people are going to die out there if we don't do something soon."

The building vibrates again as another explosion is heard in the distance. We hustle up a stairwell, gripping our weapons tighter and expecting a confrontation at any moment. A security door appears ahead as we move onto a landing. I pump a dart into my rifle from the attached magazine.

"Can you get us through it Rico?" Diago inquires.

"Got a passkey right here." He swipes the key and enters a pass code. The door pops open as the finale digit is pressed.

Kurt kicks the door open taking aim into the area beyond the door. He begins to step forward when a gunshot is fired from the other side striking the door. PING! Carlos grabs Kurt, nearly pulling him out of his shoes. "Sorry amigo. They're gunning for ya!"

Carlos quickly leaps through the door sliding across the floor with his gun aimed in the direction of the oncoming bullet. He quickly unloads two darts, engaging the gun to chamber a third. From behind the wall, we here two bodies hit the floor. He motions with his hand. "It's safe amigos." He sits up in a crouched position keeping the weapon aimed and ready for another confrontation. We enter and find two security guards face down on the floor.

"Rico. Which way do we go now?" I say with a bit of impatience in my voice.

"It's the second corridor, about halfway down on the right."

"Someone grabs those weapons. We may just need them after all."

Jim and Kurt pick up the guard's weapons as we continue. We make it to a glass window that displays a view of the bay. Looking across the land toward the ocean, we notice the flash off of battle ships pounding artillery shells at distant ships. A ship in the distance is seen burning. Smoke billows from its decks. The ocean is scattered with ships and vessels firing away with their own weaponry.

"We've got to stop this!" Diago yelps as we watch in horror.

"Come on, let's move!" I break-out into a trot, making my way quickly towards the second hall. As I round a corner, I startle three guards making their way towards me. I quickly aim and begin firing darts, pumping new ones into the gun as fast as I can pull the trigger. Bullets begin to take chunks out of the walls around me as I continue to storm at them. Two of them fall forward as the last one takes aim on me. I jam my finger on the trigger one more time as a bullet whistle by my ear. He slumbers forward with a dart hanging from his cheek. He falls as his weapon sprawls out in front of him.

Kurt comes running up from the rear. "Damn! You showed them whose boss!"

I look up at Kurt with my heart pounding from the adrenalin. "We can't stop!" I continue to dash down the hall and make the last turn towards the room. I yell to my rear, "Get Jim up here with his explosives."

I stop in front of a door with security locks on the front. Rico and Kurt catch up to me as I fumble with one lock. "Is this where they have her?"

"That's the room! They've been pressing her for information. I've been able to get food to her when she's alone."

A few of the others including Jim dash up to us. "Jim! Can you blow the door without harming anyone behind it?"

"Give me twenty seconds and the door is history." He pulls out three small charges, placing them on the hinge plates of the door. He places a forth larger unit on the lock connecting the four together with wire at connecting tabs.

"Get back! This sucker is about to come off its hinges!"

We drop behind Jim as he flips on a remote triggering device. "If you want to keep your hearing. Better plug your ears."

Everyone hunches down with fingers pressed up against their ear canals. Jim looks back to check everyone's readiness. His thumb triggers the remote. KA-WOOF! The flash brightens the hallway for a second, while the door falls forward. Smoke lingers around the entrance as I begin to step over the door. I gaze through the opening, watching for hostile activity.

"Tony!" Catalina sits tied to a chair with tears pouring from her eyes.

"My God! What have they done to you?" I run up to her placing both of my hands on each side of her head. I look into her eyes and see the anguish she has suffered. I quickly begin untying her hands and arms. She springs from the chair wrapping her arms around me in a powerful grip.

"I thought I would never see you again!" She sobs as I grip her in an embrace, I don't ever want to release.

Diago walks up and places his hand on the back of her head. "My little girl. My poor brave little girl."

She sobs harder pulling him tight to her side. "Is mom ok?"

"She's fine. These men are going to pay dearly for the pain they caused."

"It's not President Meranse. They've had him locked up in the room next door."

I look back at Jim, ordering, "Blow that door down. Let's get him out of there! He can put a halt to this whole battle!"

Jim hustles out of the room with Malik to guard his back. He pulls several more charges from his satchel on the way out.

I look at Catalina's wrists and arms noticing abrasions. "What did they do to you?"

"They slapped me around trying to get me to divulge where all of you are operating from. I told them nothing!"

"Who are they?"

"Stanovich and three of his close followers. They want the lottery to continue. They're making fortunes selling the land that remains after everyone is dead. The president is not part of it!"

I question her in a confused state, "I watched the president on television make his speech to the nation. He passed the lottery into law."

"That wasn't him. It's a computer simulation of his old speeches made to appear as if he were making them. They've had him under lock and key for months."

Suddenly, an explosion from the hall shakes the room. Jim has blown down the door of the room next to this one. I help Catalina up as we make it through the hallway. The door to the adjacent room is on the hall floor and smoke lingers around the entrance. We enter, to find Jim and Kurt helping President Meranse to his feet.

"Sir, are you all right?" I ask, watching him slowly establish his stance.

"My legs are a bit cramped from being held here. Thank God all of you came to my rescue."

"Actually, until a few minutes ago, we had set out to make sure you spent the rest of your life in prison. Is it true, they simulated your image to announce this catastrophe?"

"I've been a prisoner in this room for almost a year. I never thought I would see the light of day again."

"There's a battle going on as we speak. I need you to announce a cease-fire immediately!"

"I'll do better than that. Get me to my communication center and I'll have that bastard Stanovich hunted down. I'll stop this battle quickly!" He notices Diago holding onto Catalina. "Diago, I never thought I would be glad to have you here."

"Senor, your government has been a disgrace for too long. It's time to clean house!"

"You're absolutely right. I need your leadership to keep us on the right track."

"We can talk later. Let's put an end to all this now."

I turn to Catalina and Diago. "Make sure the President makes his broadcast. I'll take a few men to hunt down Stanovich before he gets away." I glance around the room. "Kurt, Carlos, Malik, Alonzo, Steve, Rico, and Jim come with me. The rest of you, help Diago and Catalina get Meranse to his communication center."

Catalina runs over to me and whispers in my ear, "We've been apart too long. Please be careful. A day hasn't gone by without wishing I was with you."

I grab onto her in a tight embrace. "I promise you, I'll make up to you for all of this!" I reluctantly let her go with a kiss.

We file out of the room, each group going in separate directions. Rico leads us towards the main conference center. We scramble along corridors, heading in the direction of Stanovich's main conference room, our weapons held tightly ready for immediate use. Rico motions us towards the entrance.

In front of us, a huge double door blocks entry to the U.N. officials we seek. They know this coup will end their reign on the government. I suspect they will try anything to escape or resist. The door is bolted shut from the inside with steel security bolts, making it hard for us to break it down.

"Use that assault rifle and begin blasting the locks if they won't come out!" Kurt yells to Carlos.

"Wait! Give them a chance to surrender before we create a bloodbath," I implore.

"Open this door now or I swear we'll blow it off its hinges!" Kurt bellows out of frustration.

Activity can be heard behind the door as we slowly back away. We glance back and forth at each other not knowing what to expect.

"Don't shoot. I'm going to open the door," a voice behind the door shouts.

The main latch slides into the unlock position. The door slowly opens disclosing one of Diago's men. He motions for us to enter the room. We cautiously enter, keeping our guns ready to fire. Several guards stand firmly with their arms in a surrendering stance. Several of the Vice Presidents are seated at a large conference table with looks of despair on their faces.

"Where is Stanovich?" I ask gazing over the men around the room. "I'm not in a mood to ask again!"

He's in the next room. He'll only let one of you enter," remarks a gentleman at the table.

"I glance back at my comrades. "We'll partner, I guess I'm your man." I step forward towards a door leading into the adjacent room.

"Without your weapons!"

I stop and toss my gun to Kurt. A guard walks up to me, indicating the necessity to pat me down for hidden weapons. I grudgingly raise my arms, allowing him to search my torso. Satisfied, he walks over and taps on the door. It creaks open, allowing me to enter. Across the room Stanovich sits in a large chair facing my direction. Several people stand on both sides of him watching my movements. His smug look with hair slicked back gives him a gangster like appearance. His suit obviously costs more than the gold watch gleaming on his wrist. It's startling how he resembles the old gangster Al Capone.

"So, you're one of the shit heads that screwed up my operation." He barks siz- ing me up with his beady eyes.

"No! I'm the one who's going to rip the balls off your torso!"

The man to his right lunges forward towards me snarling like a mad dog. "Hold it!" He chuckles to himself. "Don't rip him apart yet. He wants to get a rise out of me."

"You murdered thousands of innocent people to profit from their land! You really are toilet scum!" I spite bitterly.

A bodyguard rushes forward with his fists clenched as I duck downward punching upward and forward. My right fist makes contact with his throat causing him to collapse forward on the floor. He struggles to take a breath with his hands clenching his throat. I step backward, waiting for the next individual to rush me.

"I said stop!" Stanovich hollers, watching his bodyguard struggle to breathe. "Today I'll let you live. The next time I cross your path, I'm going to enjoy watching you die!" He gets up from the chair swiftly moving towards a door behind him. "You haven't heard the last of me!"

The others follow him, keeping an eye on me as they scramble through the door. I rush back to the door I came through, kicking it open with my foot. "He's escaping out the back. Throw me my rifle!" Kurt looks at me, startled by my quick entrance. He tosses the gun over to me.

"Rico! Where does that door lead to?"

"It leads up the rear stairwell to the roof. They have a helicopter waiting for them. If we hurry, we can stop them from getting away!"

"Alonzo, keep an eye on everyone in this room while we get Stanovich," I instruct.

We run through the room, following Rico. Kurt signals three others to remain with Alonzo and secure the room. A hallway at the back of the room takes us to a stairwell. As we begin to head up the stairwell, we hear the sound of a helicopter starting its motor. We pick up the pace, nearly tearing out the arm rails as we run up the stairs.

Within thirty seconds, a door appears leading to the roof. The door opens with a hard kick to the knob. The sound of the helicopter rotors accelerates as we hustle onto the rooftop. Toward the center of the roof a helicopter raises off the surface.

"They're lifting off! We're too late!" Kurt yells as he stumbles out of the door.

The helicopter lifts skyward as the rotors spin even faster. A feeling of panic comes over me as the helicopter lifts away. The side door of the helicopter remains partially open with a gun barrel protruding from it.

"They haven't gotten away yet," I exclaim watching the copter roll to the right. "Throw me a flare gun!"

Carlos quickly pulls out the flare pistol that Steve supplied. He tosses it over to me. With careful aim, I fire two flares at the helicopter. The first deflects off the window. The second flare ricochets against the inner door landing directly inside the copter. It begins to burn with extreme intensity as we watch from the roof. The pilot steers erratically as the glow inside burns brighter. We watch as the helicopter spins out of control, heading off of the roof toward the ocean. The door opens up and one individual leaps out, falling to his death. The helicopter begins to swing around wildly as the pilot struggles to control. Carlos fires one more flare ahead of the helicopter to finish off the pilot's ability to maneuver. It heads downward toward the rocky coast. Within seconds it strikes the rocks and explodes into a massive fireball, killing everyone on board. The last flare streaks off in the distance, glowing brightly as the helicopter burns on the rocky coast. I stare at the distant wreckage as a feeling of relief comes over me. The lottery just died with Stanovich.

"There's nothing more we can do here partners. Rico, take us to the communication center. Let's find out if Meranse called a cease fire. I don't hear any artil- lery shelling."

"Hombre, that's some nice shooting!" Carlos reflects staring out at the downed helicopter.

"It's over people!" Kurt revels, slapping my shoulder in a friendly gesture.

"Stanovich and his goons took the easy way out. If it had been up to me, I would have enjoyed seeing them suffer like the people did on the Yucatan Peninsula. This situation could have easily escalated into a full-scale war of immense proportions."

Together, we walk back through the door, working our way back into the building. Rico leads us down through the corridors into the main communication network area for the United Nations. I notice Catalina sitting beside President Meranse being treated for her abrasions. President Meranse is conversing with staff guards as to the people who need to be arrested and charged with various crimes. Diago is the first to notice all of us coming through the door. "What happened to Stanovich?"

"He caught a red-hot chopper to hell!" I exclaim.

"This will be a day the world can celebrate! All of you can be very proud of yourselves. You made history today!"

The President looks over at all of us with smile on his face. "Every one of you will be greatly rewarded for all you have accomplished. The world owes you a tre- mendous debt of gratitude."

"Partner, just take care of the people affected by this lottery. There's a lot of people hurting out there. Make sure they get food from now on."

"A lot of things in this government are going to change. Starting with the food program."

"Just to keep things honest, Diago Delray needs to be your secondhand VP. He'll keep things secure around here." I say, as I wink at Diago.

"I always wondered why General Delray rejected this government. Now I see why." President Meranse hesitates for a second to think. "I will need you, if you want the position."

"Only if I can bring aboard Tony and his people in positions of my choosing."

"Of course! Anything you need."

I jump into the conversation at this juncture, "Whoa now! I need time to think about that. I've got some friends that need a partner in a bar in Cancun. They tell me the area is going to need some work. I may just need to help with that." I wink at Kurt and Carlos as I pick Catalina up in my arms. "General Delray, I would like to ask you for your permission to marry your daughter!"

Catalina shrieks with excitement, "Tony! Yes! Yes!" She begins to sob. "I'm so in love with you!"

"Of course you have my permission. I'd be proud to have you in the family." Diago exclaims.

The others howl with congratulations as I carry Catalina to a more comfortable setting. Kurt contacts Kyle on the radio and acknowledges our success. News journalists begin to pour into the building, taking photos and gathering information about the coup. The world has a new reason to rejoice. This day will become a day of celebration. It marks an end to the bloody lottery.

C H A P T E R   17

RECOVERY

Diago begins his interrogation of the elected officials of the United Nations. Seven of the remaining vice presidents are handcuffed and led away to face charges. Government conspiracy and corruption are just a few of the criminal charges facing them. Their crimes will be the center of many discussions in the days ahead. Diago Delray is hard at work attempting to get the government in Iceland back on track. Reorganization is going to take time, but the right man is on the job.

Military and naval ships are ordered back to their posts, allowing ships in our armada to return to their countries of origin. In all, four ships were destroyed. Two from Spain, one from the United States, and one from Canada. Two-hundred-and-fifty-six men lost their lives in the sea battle. Another three-hundred-and-sixty-three fell victim to injuries. The critically injured are flown out to hospitals in Norway, France, and Spain. Some of the ships remain in the area to help out with the restructuring and cleanup.

Celebrations are held worldwide, hailing us as conquering heroes. Ships can be heard all over blasting their fog horns and firing flares. The world has a lot to celebrate. The lottery will never take another life.

Kyle docks the submarine at the base in Iceland. He and the remaining crew turn it over to officials within the military. It is eventually returned to the United States in North Carolina to remain on display for the world to see. The stealth system is secretly taken off by Steve and dismantled without being discovered.

The sub is docked and a new chapter written into its history. A plaque is erected in our honor, giving a brief history as to the sub's newest exploits.

The media is tearing down walls to interview us and gather information about our operation. We steer clear of as many reporters as possible. Information is filtered down to them in the proper channels, allowing us to recuperate after our ordeal. All of us just want to return to our normal lives with a government that makes sense.

Secretly, we all get out of Iceland leaving the cleanup to the proper individuals. We board a Navy transport aircraft and head to Jamaica. The aircraft is the safest way for us to leave without running into the media.

Upon arriving in Jamaica, we find the Sea Jewel fit and ready for a relaxing voyage. In Jamaica the people recognize us and the celebration continues. People gather along the docks and cheer for us as we prepare the ship to cast off. Malik is in his glory as the Sea Jewel takes on a new persona. He waves at his old neighbors with new vigor as we all make the last preparations. We pull the ropes and start the diesels making our way out of port. Our new direction is Starpoint Island.

The voyage is one of relaxation and comfort. For the first time in many months, we relax and celebrate without a care in the world. The Sea Jewel plunges along with the crew and passengers partying with vigor. Catalina and I take the most comfortable room available and disappear often to make love with electrifying passion.

As we pull around to the lagoon, everyone can be seen waving and cheering along the shoreline. The celebration is just starting. We plan to commemorate the end of the lottery. None of us have a care in the world as we laugh and reminisce about the whole campaign. The night seems magical. It's hard to believe we can go on with our lives. I can't remember a time when the future seems as bright as it does today.

It takes a few days to gather up our belongings and transfer them to the Sea Jewel. Steve dismantles the stealth system and packs it away. The small sub and the boats are set on the deck of the ship. By the fourth day, we leave Starpoint Island and head back to Cancun.

We arrive in Cancun to find the area busy with activity. Funerals are being held as people try to adjust to the terrible tragedy that took place on the peninsula. People recognize us and the emotions are indescribable. We make our way to the Casa' de la Parrot and find it in great shape. People in the area have decorated the outside of the bar in honor of our arrival. Many people bring wreaths and pictures of their lost loved ones to display on the walkway outside the bar.

They are an eerie reminder of what took place not too long ago. It's a feeling that will take all of us time to get over.

We immediately begin restoring the bar. The government, thanks to Diago Delray, begins pouring money into the Yucatan Peninsula. Funds are allocated to the families of the victims who were lost due to the lottery. Reorganization will take us through some tough times, but the world will never have to face a tragedy like this one again. Everyone involved promises to keep Starpoint a complete secret. We never know when it may be needed in the future.

The wedding will take place soon after we have had reasonable time to recover. Within days Malik announces the wedding plans of Juanita and himself. We decide a double ceremony is the only way to celebrate an occasion as great as this. Catalina makes Malik promise there will be no practical jokes during the affair. He reluctantly agrees, but with Malik anything can happen.

Our operation has succeeded in triggering reorganization of the United Nations Government. Diago Delray remains in Iceland to help restructure and get to the truth about the corruption of the government. He acknowledges to us his plans to run for the presidency.